The Adventures of

Jesus Christ, Boy Detective

J. Bradley

Jesus Christ, Boy Detective by J. Bradley

ISBN-10: 1938349407
ISBN: 978-1-938349-40-9
eISBN: 978-1-938349-45-4
Library of Congress Control Number: 2016932275

"Philadelphia" and "Black & Blue"
        previously appeared in *MungBeing* (2012)
"From the Hips"
        previously appeared in *Go Read Your Lunch* (2013)
"Draining Chutes, Ladders"
        previously appeared in *The Flash Future Review* (2012)
"The Early Bird Gets The Shaft"
        previously appeared in *Whole Beast Rag* (2012)
"The Freshly Squeezed Slugger"
        previously appeared in *Paragraph Line* (2013)
portions of "The Hand of Fate"
        previously appeared in *Unshod Quills* (2012)
        and *The Fiddleback* (2013)

Layout and Book Design by Mark Givens
First Pelekinesis Printing 2016

For information:
Pelekinesis, 112 Harvard Ave #65, Claremont, CA 91711 USA

www.pelekinesis.com

Jesus Christ,
Boy Detective

J. Bradley

PRAISE FOR *THE ADVENTURES OF JESUS CHRIST, BOY DETECTIVE* BY J. BRADLEY

"Gloriously weird. Beautifully savage. J. Bradley's stories are absolute marvels. He writes like a person riding a comet down from a brand new illustrated outer space. Pure wonder. *Jesus Christ, Boy Detective* is his most stunning work. Every page is rich with fireworks bursting up signaling a call to adventure."

—Bud Smith, author of *F250*

"J. Bradley's *The Adventures of Jesus Christ, Boy Detective* is my new Bible—a wickedly bizarre page turner from a whip smart storyteller."

—John Jodzio, author of the short story collections *Knockout* and *If You Lived Here You'd Already Be Home*

"In *Jesus Christ, Boy Detective*, J. Bradley mercilessly crucifies the kid detective genre we loved as children and resurrects it with the Living God himself as the ultimate existential child sleuth. It's impossible to have read something like this before because nothing like it has ever been written."

—Rion Amilcar Scott, author of *Insurrections*

"It may sound odd to compare a book about Jesus trapped in a boy detective's body to work by Haruki Murukami, but that's immediately where I went after reading this weird, wild, wonderful thing that J. Bradley has made. Funny, formally innovative, and full of misdirection and literary sleight of hand, this is a once in a blue moon book that every writer should read, if only to remember that originality lives on despite recent reports to the contrary."

—Amber Sparks, author of *The Unfinished World And Other Stories*

"With the pace and tension of the final hand in a game of high-stakes poker, J. Bradley's *The Adventures of Jesus Christ, Boy Detective* is breathless fiction that adores and destroys genre in the same embrace. Whether you call it iconoclastic or call it plain old god-bothering, don't ever think you're safe (or saved) because you think you 'get it.' I promise you don't. One of the most satisfying endings I've read in years."

—Laura Ellen Scott, author of *The Juliet* and *Death Wishing*

To my wife, Laura.
Thank you for always letting me be a little
weird.

Contents

Prelude

The Hand of Fate

Mathias looked at the cards in his hand: three 4s (♦, ♣, ♠), an Ace ♥ and a King ♠, then glanced at Joseph. "I'm all in." Mathias pushed his chips into the pot.

"Call," Joseph shoved all his chips into the pot, then crushed Mathias's three-of-a-kind with a full house—three 7s (♥, ♦, ♣) and a pair of Queens (♥, ♠). "It looks like you're out of the game."

"God dam…" The petrification started with his mouth, spreading to his face, shirt, suspenders, pants, boots, until a statue of Mathias sat in his place.

The chair legs groaned as Daniel pushed himself away from the poker table. "What the fuck is going on here? What kind of fuckin' game is this?" Henry buried his face in his hands, smudging his spectacles with clammy palms. Frank took a flask out of the inner pocket of his worn gray duster.

"This is gonna be a long night," Frank said after a pull.

* * *

Henry Wormwood stood next to a freshly covered grave, alone. He baked in his black bowler hat and sack suit, face swollen from grief.

"I'm sorry for your loss." The sentence sneaked through Henry's sobs. Henry turned around to see a figure, cloaked and hooded in white.

"Who…are…you?" The figure handed Henry a handkerchief. Henry cleaned his spectacles, blew his nose.

"What are you willing to do to get this person back?"

"I can't get them back. No one can do that."

"What if I can?"

* * *

"I'm done with this! Deal me the fuck out!" Daniel yelled. He took five steps away from the poker table before a lightning bolt struck where he would have taken the sixth step.

Only one will be allowed to leave this table.

Frank drew the sawed-off double barreled shotgun out of his duster. "Who's there?" The cards in Joseph's hands began humming, the pitch growing louder. Frank clutched his head, Daniel his stomach, Henry's glasses cracked. "Joseph, what did you just do?" Frank pointed his shotgun at Joseph's chest.

"Nothin', I swear to God, nothin'."

"Frank, he's right." Henry said, putting his hand on Frank's left shoulder. "It's this game. Strange things have happened at the end of each hand. There's something about those cards."

"When I lost my showdown against Frank, I couldn't see out of my right eye for a coupla hands," Daniel said.

"Mathias said he lost that limp he had after winning a hand," Joseph said. "But why did he die?"

"How did we get the chips?" Henry rubbed his chin, "We didn't get an equal amount either. Some got more some got less." Henry looked at the other men. Frank was in his mid-40s, a scar running like a tear beneath his left eye. You couldn't tell Joseph had wrinkles until he smiled. Daniel's cheeks looked like they were slapped by the doctor after birth.

Only one will be allowed to leave this table.

* * *

Joseph's back was to the wall. Four bad hands, two bluffs later, he was down to his last few chips. In the showdown against Henry, his two pair—Aces (♥, ♦) and

10s (♠, ♦)—lost to a straight—5, 6, 7 (♠), 8 ♦, 9 ♥. Joseph's last pose was his hands clasped in prayer. Frank couldn't move his left arm.

* * *

Daniel was ahead in the chip count, Henry second, Frank third, slowly losing more and more chips after each round.

"Hot damn, I'm gonna win this whole thing," Daniel yelled. "I'm gonna get cleared of the charges and go home to my wife."

"Whareyoutalkin'about," Henry slurred. The last hand he lost paralyzed the left side of his body.

"I was told if I won then what I did on the train is gonna go away. I'll get to go back to my family, my little girl. You are almost done, old man. Then it's just between me and the yellow belly. I'm gonna beat the Dutch, just you wait." After his final showdown, the shotgun dropped out of Frank's hand before he had a chance to fire at Daniel. His arm stayed outstretched. Henry picked the gun off the floor and opened the barrels.

"Daniel, I think Frank was the man they called Eureka in the papers a while back. The barrels are full of pyrite, 'Fool's Gold'. He was the scourge of the Union army. Killed 120 men before going into hiding after the war was over. Wasn't even a solider, just a vigilante. Before he shot someone, he yelled 'Eureka'."

"That's horseshit, Frank, horseshit. Now, sit down and let's get this finished. Got a wife and a little girl waiting for me."

* * *

After the next few hands, Henry's glasses looked brand new, Daniel coughed and wheezed every so often. The chip count on both sides looked fairly even. Daniel's last hand was a Jack-high flush (♦). Henry shuffled and dealt. Daniel looked at his hand and smiled.

"I'm goin' all in."

"Are you sure you want to do that, Daniel?"

"Hell yeah, I am. I won with a flush last hand. Diamonds. Every time one of us won with lots of Diamonds in their hand, somethin' mighty good happened. I've got a good feelin' about this hand."

Henry pushed all of his chips in the middle of the table. "Call."

"Read 'em and weep. A straight, Queen high." After Daniel saw Henry's hand, he froze, mouth puckered in 'no'.

"Well done." The figure cloaked and hooded and white walked toward Henry. "You have one more hand to play." The green felt table cloth from the poker table disappeared, revealing a pentacle carved into the table top and a new stack of chips. *Only one will be allowed to leave this table.* The figure took off the hood, revealing slicked back black hair, dull brown eyes, a Roman nose, and a weak jawline. "Hello, Henry. That was a nice funeral you did for me."

"How did you…"

"A potion that simulates death. Two days after I died, my assistant dug me up and revived me. He was the one who gave you the last invitation to the game. You were the last ingredient."

"Last ingredient for what?"

"To unleash the true apocalyptic power of the deck, I need the life force of five sinners of different degrees. Daniel was a thief, Joseph was a grifter, Mathias molested little girls, Frank was a killer, and you laid with men."

"But I thought you loved me, Benjamin."

"You were just a pawn for a greater good." There was a loud bang, then blood spilled from Henry's ruptured back before collapsing. Daniel held the smoking shotgun.

"You fuckin' Sodomite. I hope you burn in Hell for what you've done." Daniel spit on Henry's face.

"What have you done?" Benjamin yelled as he pointed at Daniel. His index finger shivered.

"What are you tryin' to do, poke me to death?"

"No." Benjamin thrust his arm again, his index finger strained. "No. You've broken the pact." The poker table cracked. The ground beneath fissured, the broken table falling into the earth. Daniel aimed the shotgun at Benjamin. Click.

"I'm glad I used both barrels on your friend. What you've got comin' is gonna be far worse."

"We're going to the same place, you know."

"Yeah, well I'm ready to pay for my sins. I reckon you aren't." Daniel watched Benjamin fall before the ground gave way beneath him. The floor righted itself, leaving only the deck of playing cards. A gray cloaked and hooded figure picked up the deck, placed it in a black tin, then put the tin in a pocket. The figure walked out of the building, never looking back.

Chapter 1

1.

Tom Hightower gripped the wheel of his pearl colored Range Rover. The rain turned the highway into a shallow, raging river. Mary Hightower peered through the windshield, looking for the exit to her mother's house. Timmy Hightower looked through his pocket notebook, trying to piece together the clues regarding the case Marie Swanson hired him for to find out who would forge a love letter in her handwriting to Carlos Francisco, Parker Lewis Middle School's token pariah.

"Mary, do you see the exit yet?" Tom sighed. The sweat slowly knitted wet gloves around his hands.

"No, I don't Tom. Why don't we just pull over and sit a

bit until the rain stops."

"We're running late as is, baby. There's no need…"

The burst of the Range Rover's right front and rear tire interrupted Tom's sentence. Tom furiously turned the wheel as the Range Rover spun out before a Mack truck tapped it just enough for it to flip and roll until it stopped, wheels spinning in the air. The horn cried like a dirge as a figure in a raincoat walked over to the ruined Range Rover.

"Hhheeellp…hellllp ssusss." Tom's broken ribs fractured his plea. The figure walked to the back seat, crouched to look. The seatbelt kept Timmy in his seat, the blood trickling from his forehead onto the roof. The figure picked something shiny out of the back right tire before walking back and picking something out of the front tire. The figure crouched down, looked into Tom's desperate gray eyes before covering his mouth. Tom's arms wanted to move, slap the figure's wrist. Tom's eyes fluttered, his body slacked.

"The vessel is ready." The figure said to the rain.

"Good." The rain hissed back. "You have done well."

* * *

"How…is he doing?" Leopold Franz's question came out in a faint German/Christopher Walken drawl. The night nurse stared at the man's slicked back black hair, salt and pepper handlebar mustache, the tattoo creeping from the collar of his shirt.

"Who are you?"

"I'm…his uncle."

The night nurse stared harder, her brow furrowing. Her cheeks quivered, trying hard to fight her fear, her awkward surprise. "Wait, you're…"

"I am, yes."

"Pardon me for asking but how are you related to the Hightowers?"

"Every family…has a wolf…they'd rather forget." Leopold tackled the night nurse as the lightning bolt came through the window and struck Timmy Hightower. The EKG flattened, moaned. "Are…you ok?" Leopold helped the night nurse up.

"I am. Thank you." The night nurse noticed the monotone of the EKG. She punched a button over Timmy's head. The loudspeakers chanted "Code Blue, Code Blue, Code Blue." Doctors, nurses, ran past Leopold.

"Sir, you'll need to wait in the waiting room. We'll let you know what happened when we're done."

Leopold turned, walking calmly from Timmy Hightower's hospital room, into the nearest men's room. He looked around to make sure he was alone before running the water and dunking his face. *I know you know what you're doing,* Leopold thought to himself. *I hope one day…I understand.*

2.

Three of the playing cards laid face up on the kitchen table (8 ♥, King ♠, King ♦). A charcoal pinstriped suited man peeked at his cards before looking back at the 12-year-old boy. The boy ran his tongue across his braces, peeking at his cards slightly.

"You've played well so far, Larry. So well, far better than I thought you would. It's a shame this game has to end."

"Dude, are you gonna shut up or are you gonna make the turn?"

The charcoal pinstriped suited man slipped his hand beneath one of the face down cards in the middle of the kitchen table, revealing it as a King ♥.

"This is quite interesting. Your move, Larry."

Larry's chips glowed brighter as he pushed them all into the rest of the pile. "I'm all in, dude. You got the balls to follow me in or are you gonna fold like a pussy?" The charcoal pinstriped suited man's chips glowed just as bright as he pushed all of them into the pile.

"It's time to see what the river brings." The fifth card is an Ace ♠. "Call." Larry revealed an Ace ♥ and a 5 ♣.

"Full house, dude, Aces and Kings. Think you can beat that?" The charcoal pinstriped suited man revealed a King ♣ and a 7 ♥. Blood trickled out of Larry's mouth, each drop that touched his skin turned it to stone.

"Wghah ghav yoah don to me?"

"The same thing you just did to your friends. You all knew the stakes going in."

The blood poured faster out of Larry's mouth, stone creeping up his body until he was a statue sitting at the head of his family's dining room table. The chips melded into a column of light, shattering the ceiling above. The charcoal pinstriped suited man collected the cards, placed them in a black tin, then sealed it tight. He didn't look back at the other statues sitting at the table as he left Larry's house.

You did well, Nathaniel. The words buzzed in the charcoal pinstriped suited man's ears as he walked to the faded midnight black Camry parked adjacent to the outside curb of Larry's house. Nathaniel opened the driver's side door of his Camry, settled in the driver's seat before putting in the keys. The local talk radio station played the news about the death of the Hightower family, of Timmy Hightower still struggling to wake up from his coma.

Nathaniel, start finding players for the next game.

"This quickly? We need to lay low for awhile."

Make it happen, Nathaniel. Do you understand? Nathaniel nodded as he turned the ignition, set the Camry to D, and drove normally out of Larry's neighborhood.

* * *

"How's the father doing?"

"Not so well. He had to be sedated and taken to the hospital. You wouldn't be doing that well either if you found his kid and four of his friends…"

"How did they do it though, Chief? Did each kid slit the others wrist and then watched each other die? Where's all the blood?"

"All of these are good questions. This is just too damn weird for our detectives to handle. I mean, they'll have to try and figure out what happened. It's their job, but I don't think they'll solve this. I might need some outside help."

"Outside help? Like FBI?"

"No. I think I'm staying local on this one."

"Wait. If you're thinking who I'm thinking, this might even be too weird for him. Besides, he…"

"I know. I know. I hope he makes it. We need him more than ever."

3.

Leopold Franz watched Timmy Hightower's eyes flutter beneath his eyelids before snapping open.

"You're…awake. Thank God. I thought…I lost you."

"Where…am I?"

"You're at…St. Joseph's. You, your mom, and dad… got into a really bad accident on the highway."

"But my mom's already dead and my dad is…"

Leopold placed a finger to Timmy's lips. "Good… you're in there. I need you to…relax. In a minute or two, the night nurse is going to come in and check on you. You…need to act like the boy as best as you can."

"Why should I trust you?"

"Because he's asked me…to make sure I watch over you while you are in this body."

"I can escape this body. Watch." Timmy Hightower gritted his teeth, clenched his fists, shut his eyes. The EKG beeped faster. Timmy opened his eyes and noticed that he was still tethered to his hospital bed. "Why isn't this working? Why am I here? What have you done," Timmy asked the ceiling.

"We've got about…thirty seconds. The boy's memories…are intact. Access them…and use them. You'll need to play along…in order to get out of here."

"Why?"

"Do you trust me?"

"I don't have a choice, do I?"

"You do. If you say who you really are though, it'll be written off…as brain damage. You'll be in here…a lot longer." Leopold heard the sneakers of the night nurse squeaking closer. "Well?"

Timmy closed his eyes again, thrashed beneath his eyelids before opening again. "Uncle Leo, is that you? What happened?"

"Timmy, thank God. I thought...I lost you. You, your mom, and dad...got into a really bad accident on Highway 27."

"Are...they ok? Where are they?"

The night nurse walked into Timmy's hospital room, watched Leopold take Timmy's hand into his. She held back her own tears as a slowly sobbing Timmy dived into Leopold's chest, Leopold's shirt muffling Timmy's questions, snot and wails.

* * *

The boy is awake now. You know what to do.

Nathaniel took five random playing cards from the black tin, placed each one in a white envelope, then sealed them. The mailing addresses slowly appeared in gold cursive, with a subtle crimson outline around each letter. He placed a Forever Stamp on each envelope, then stacked them in a neat pile. Nathaniel placed them in his inner pocket before walking out of the motel room, to the mailbox at the front of the hotel, feeding it the envelopes.

4.

Timmy and Leopold sat in the left front pew of the viewing room, listening to the priest giving Timmy's mother and father their eulogy. Timmy heard the pew behind them creak as a new person slid in. Over his shoulder, Timmy noticed the new person in a formal police uniform, the length and width of his black beard, and the mahogany pipe sticking out of his left breast pocket. He leaned into Timmy's right ear.

"I'm so sorry for your loss, Tim. This was terribly tragic," the man whispered. Timmy shut his eyes for a moment.

"Yes. Yes, Chief Donaldson, it was." Timmy numbed the words.

"Is there anything I can do for you, at all, anything?"

"I don't think so, Chief."

Chief Donaldson began scooting out of the pew before leaning into Timmy's ear again. "I hate to do this to you but there's a case I need your help on."

"Chief, my mom and dad just died. Can't this wait a few days?"

"This can't wait a few days. I'll talk to you after the burial, ok?"

"What is so damn important...about this case?" Leopold hissed. Chief Donaldson pulled out a manilla folder, handed it to Timmy.

"Once you look in here, you'll understand."

* * *

Timmy, Leopold, and Chief Donaldson walked through Larry Kreg's parents' house, ignoring the lazy '70s decor and color choice. They stopped in the dining room.

"Why do you need me for this again, Chief? The file

said murder/suicide. This is something your CSI team should be walking through, not a twelve-year-old boy."

"We had to put something down, Tim. Didn't you read through all the report?"

"Yeah…there wasn't any blood found and…" Timmy looked up at the plastic tarp bandaging the hole in the roof above the dining room table.

"You've dealt with weird cases before and we're all stumped on how all of this happened. A murder/suicide without any traces of blood. A giant hole in the roof but no gunpowder or traces of explosive chemicals. I need a fresh perspective, Tim, and you're the best option I've got."

Timmy walked around the dining room table, looking at it, ducking underneath it. He noticed Chief Donaldson's shined shoes marring a faint curve on the floor. Timmy used one of the dining room chairs to step up to the top of the dining room table.

"Chief, does your phone have a camera?"

"It does, why?"

"Throw it to me." Chief Donaldson pulled an iPhone in a police blue case, handed it to Timmy. "I need you both to step away from the dining room."

Leopold and Chief Donaldson walked out of the room. Timmy took pictures all around the dining room floor, connecting the curves of the circle in his head. *Is this why you put me here in this body? You could at least answer me.* The only thing Timmy heard in response was the built in sound effects of the camera taking picture after picture.

Chapter 2

1.

"Peter, how has the boy adjusted thus far?"

"He's still disoriented over the whole thing."

"What have you told him?"

"Nothing yet. He keeps asking if his mom and dad are ok, which would make sense because he thinks he's sitting in a waiting room at the hospital, waiting to find out if they'll be ok."

"Good."

2.

Timmy cut the curves out of the photos, piecing them together in Adobe Photoshop.

"For someone… who's been dead for a long time… you look just like him doing that." Leopold stood at the bottom step of Timmy's basement office/crime lab.

"I've picked up on how to use this body quickly. I tried asking my father why I was here and he's not answering.

Do you know why I'm here, Leopold?" Leopold walked over to an empty office chair, slumping into it.

"He only told me…to keep you safe."

"Did he at least tell you how long I'm here in this body for?"

"No. What…is that?" Leopold pointed at the monitor.

"This was why I got on the dining room table. I asked Larry's father if that was originally there and he shook his head. The circumference and diameter of the circle on the floor match the circumference and diameter of the hole in the roof." Timmy punched a couple of buttons on the keyboard. "When you look closer, the circle looks entirely burned into the floor but in a way where the splinters point up. Yet, the dining room table and chairs are completely intact."

"What…are you saying?"

"Something Larry and his friends were doing caused this to happen."

"What…now?"

Timmy crooked his head down, rubbing his chin. "We pay a visit to the house across the street from Larry's."

* * *

"You…realize…someone hasn't lived in this house… for awhile."

Timmy and Leopold stood outside the baby blue colored house, the thick grass swallowing their calves.

"Damn…I mean darn it, Uncle Leo."

"It's ok…you know…you are twelve. They do swear…not normally around adults…but they swear… frequently."

"I haven't…I mean I'm so used to watching everything I say because he got really pissed really quick if you said something he didn't like."

"I…can understand that. Now what?" Timmy and Leopold turned away from the foreclosed home and walked towards Leopold's cobalt blue El Camino.

"Back to the lab."

* * *

Timmy pinned a photo of each boy from the police file on the cork bulletin board perpendicular from his computer. He stepped back and stared, arms akimbo.

"Leo, I don't get it. I'm accessing Timmy's memories and the only one that I know about is Larry, who played point guard for Parker Lewis Middle School's basketball team. What do these boys all have in common?"

"Have you…read their obituaries?"

"No, have you?" Leo shook his head. "That wouldn't hurt to try that first then."

* * *

LARRY KREG, guard for the Parker Lewis Panthers basketball team, died suddenly at his home on March 7. He also played shortstop for the John Cougar Summer Camp Little League team, which made the National finals at the Little League World Series. Larry is survived by his father…"

"…**SIMON DANSON** was known for his world class clownery at Dali Junior High. We will miss him for the way he made us laugh. Simon is survived by his mother, Diane, and his stepfather, Michael…"

"The world lost a potential great in **FRANCO MORALES**, Parker Lewis' 8th Grade Class President. In the summers, he traveled to Spain to train as a future bullfighter. We are sincerely gored by this tragic loss but are grateful that he finally will join his mother and father in Heaven, making his family whole once again…"

"**DON MAT** was a *Magic: the Gathering* collector and the president of the costume play club at Mel Blanc Middle School. He is survived by his father, Salvadore Mat."

"Our angel, **Brandon Johnson**, was called home by the Lord on March 7. He is survived by his uncle, Don, and his aunt, Frances."

Timmy rubbed his eyes. For the first time in a long time, he understood fatigue and hunger, his head throbbed. "Leo!" Timmy yelled up the stairs.

"Yes?" Leopold yelled back.

"Do we have anything to eat? I'm…hungry! Really hungry now that I've started thinking about it!"

"Not…really. Also…I'm not that much of a cook."

"Darn."

"We…can go somewhere, though."

"Where?"

"Look within and you'll see."

* * *

Timmy and Leopold sat outside of Taco Dog. Timmy savored Taco Dog's patented red hot chili cheese taco dog, flecks of liquid cheese staining the corner of his mouth and chin. The taco shaped dog stood on its hind legs, holding a fat bright yellow and red sign touting their kennel of regular Taco Dogs for just five dollars.

"Why do I like this so much?"

"Timmy…always ate one of these things to help jog his memory. He said…"

"…the burning feeling in his stomach makes his focus sharper on a really difficult case."

"Exactly."

Timmy took a napkin and wiped his mouth. He picked up the cup full of Mr. Pibb and dulled the lake of hot dairy in his throat before pulling out the obituaries. "So far we can rule out the school connection since most of them went to different middle schools."

"And…age…they were all in middle schools but in different grade levels."

"Right. Their activities were even different. Why would a jock, a class clown, a future bullfighter, a nerd, and a nobody be hanging out at the same house." Timmy placed the obituaries on the table, stood up and looked at them. He removed his mechanical pencil from his left pocket and began circling each obituary in specific areas. "That's it! That's the connection. Uncle Leo, do you see?" Leopold stood up,

"**LARRY KREG,** guard for the Parker Lewis Panthers basketball team, died suddenly at his home on March 7. He also played shortstop for the John Cougar Summer Camp Little League team, which made the National finals at the Little League World Series. Larry is survived by his father…"

"…**SIMON DANSON** was known for his world class clownery at Dali Junior High. We will miss him for the way he made us laugh. Simon is survived by his mother, Diane, and his stepfather, Michael…"

looking over Timmy's shoulders.

"I do."

"Now we have to figure out what and why."

3.

"I don't know how much longer I can keep the waiting room at the hospital intact."

"Peter…what do you mean?"

"He's starting to notice the same number of people, how they all look the same, how the hands of the clock aren't really moving or that he's not tired or not hungry. He can sense he's been waiting for a long time but time itself isn't really moving."

"Then make it more realistic, Peter."

"How? I only have so much control and a finite amount of energy to maintain that control. I'd ask you to help but even you…"

"Even I what, Peter? Even I…what?"

"You used a lot to make the switch. You could have waited

> "The world lost a potential great in **Franco Morales**, Parker Lewis' 8th Grade Class President. In the summers, he traveled to Spain to train as a future bullfighter. We are sincerely gored by this tragic loss but are grateful that he finally will join his mother and father in Heaven, making his family whole once again…"

> "**Don Mat** was a *Magic: the Gathering* collector and the president of the costume play club at Mel Blanc Middle School. He is survived by his father, Salvadore Mat."

> "Our angel, **Brandon Johnson**, was called home by the Lord on March 7. He is survived by his uncle, Don, and his aunt, Frances."

until you gathered more strength but you didn't. Why?"

"The timing was finally right. Years and years of planning this and everything fell in the right place. Soon, we'll finally get what we need. For now, you must do everything you can to make his environment more real."

"How?"

"Any wars you can get started? The freshness in our newcomers would be of tremendous help to our cause."

"Really, is that what it'll take? Haven't we done enough?"

"When you tell someone not to do something, it just encourages them to do it even more. The whole Commandments thing was never intended to be do-as-I-do, but do-as-I-say. Remember the look on their faces when he came back down from the mountain and showed them the tablets and then the earth opened up to swallow those who broke the rules? Priceless. So priceless. He was such a good operative. Shame he had to go the way he did. But I digress. Yes, Peter, this is what it will take. Pull the necessary strings and do it quickly."

"What about the boy?"

"I'll divert some of my energy to cover for you while you reach out to our operatives to get the ball rolling so we can obtain fresh souls. Will that work?" Peter nodded.

* * *

The old diving suit groaned as it craned its neck, looking up at the man in a dirty white lab coat, the earpieces of his chrome and red rubber stethoscope pinching his neck.

"Doc…how are my folks…are they doing ok?" The diving helmet muffled the cracked syllables and awkward tone inside the question.

"Timmy, they're still in a coma, we're doing everything we can."

"Where's my grandma? Why isn't she here?"

"I'll have one of the nurses try and get ahold of her. Why don't you rest for awhile?"

"I…" The diving suit collapsed, cracking the tile beneath his back.

"Good boy." The waiting room disintegrated, leaving the diving suit laying in the middle of a blank, sterile room.

4.

"Wake…up, Timmy."

Timmy lifted his head from the open desk space near his keyboard, seeing a tilted version of Leopold holding a glass of orange juice. Leopold walked over and placed it next to Timmy's face.

"What…what time is it?"

"Seven…in the morning. You've got an hour or so before you have…to get going."

Timmy sat himself upright, taking the tall glass

of orange juice in his right hand, downing it, then slamming the glass down on the table. "Going where, Uncle Leo?"

"Think...for a moment."

Timmy shut his eyes for a few moments before his eyelids flew open. "Really? I have to go? Come on, Leo."

"You've been out of school...for two weeks now... between the coma...and the funeral. The doctors said you can...return today."

"But I have a case to solve here, Leo. That takes precedence over everything."

"Timmy understood...the need to balance his caseload with his personal life and his schoolwork. Even though...this is the strangest case Timmy has ever worked on...Chief Donaldson would drag Timmy to school...personally. He has actually...a couple of times."

"Really?" Leopold nodded. "There wasn't anything like this back when I was Timmy's age. How do I do this? How do I deal with this?"

"The same way...you've been working on this case... trust in Timmy's brain. You'll...manage."

* * *

Timmy watched various boys and girls walk through the doors of Parker Lewis Middle School. Some were hanging outside, catching up on what happened last weekend. Timmy gripped the straps of his black JanSport backpack. "I can do this. I can do this."

"Timmy? Is that you?"

Timmy turned around. She had blonde hair pageboy cut, her bangs just above her eyebrows. Her brown eyes reminded him of Mary's.

"Um…yeah."

The girl lunged, wrapped her arms around him allowing Timmy to inhale the starter perfume on her neck. "Timmy…oh Timmy I'm so glad you're alive…I'm so sorry to hear about your parents." Timmy felt the tips of her fingernails caress his back. He shut his eyes.

"Yeah…Marie…yeah…I'm still processing all of this." Marie broke the hug and stepped back.

"I…can't say that I can relate, Tim. I can't. I hope that kind of things never happens to me—for my sake and for my sister's. I don't think we could handle it." Now, about the case…"

"What case?" Marie squinted, hands reaching to position themselves on her hips. "Oh…I'm sorry Marie, yeah, what about it?"

"I can understand if you need more time to crack it, with everything you are going through and all."

Timmy fought the urge to tell her to do something she probably hasn't done with someone, let alone to herself. "Um, Marie, really? 'I can understand if you need more time to crack it'?"

"Did I…oh."

"Yeah. Oh." The warning bell rang through the

loudspeakers. "Look, Marie, I have to put your case on the back burner for a bit. There's a new case that demands all of my attention. If you want your money back, I'll refund you."

Marie gripped her hips. "What case is more important than mine?"

"Larry Kreg, did you know him?" Marie relaxed her hands. Timmy looked down and closed his eyes. "Yeah, you did, didn't you? Aren't you two...I mean weren't..." Marie nodded, her eyes squeezed shut.

"Yeah. We were. He was the one who pushed to hire you to find out about that note. Do you think..."

"We've got to get to class before we get in trouble. We'll talk later." Timmy didn't wait for Marie to nod before running into the building.

5.

"How does he do this every day?" Timmy rubbed his head on his locker as the inaccuracy of Mr. Wesler's beliefs on Creationism throbbed in his brain. "What are they teaching these children?"

"You're not Timmy."

Timmy turned to the voice. He was tall and lanky, his black overcoat swallowing his body. He kept moving the hair out of his face, eyes black brown staring at Timmy.

"And you are..."

"Come on, man, don't bullshit me. I know you're not

Timmy. Who are you?"

"Is he bothering you?" A sagging linebacker appeared right next to Timmy, the yellow Polo shirt squeezing his gut. His mustache was a combination of throwback porn star and questionably friendly Pop Warner football coach.

"Really, dude, you're gonna let this whale fight your battles for you."

"Carlos…I'm warning you." The sagging linebacker breathed, huffed, clenching his fists.

"What are you warning me about? That you're gonna get all close to me and get me in the showers. I know I'm not even your type. You like 'em like you used to be, all young and athletic, in their prime. I'm too stringy for you and your mouth." The linebacker began clomping, building up speed. Carlos walked backwards briskly at first. "Come on, motherfucker. Catch me if you can." Carlos pivoted, his overcoat flapping in the breeze. The locks slapped the lockers with each running clomp of the sagging linebacker. "I'll see you again, not Timmy." The sentence echoed through the halls.

* * *

"How…was your first day at school, Timmy?" Leopold stood at his normal spot in Timmy's lab, on the bottom step. Timmy turned in his office chair to face Leopold.

"It…it was really stressful. And weird. And I'm so glad we didn't have middle school back then. All the hormones and the violence…that would have been really scary. Here's the weird thing…this kid Carlos…he said I wasn't Timmy…like he could see who I actually was. I don't quite get how though." Timmy closed his eyelids, rolled back his eyes for a moment, then opened them. "Ok, he's always been really weird, but…how could he…ok, Timmy, ok, one mystery at a time."

Timmy pulled up the photos from Larry Kreg's father's dining room, fed them to an image search site. "Let's see if this finds anything on these images."

"You…got this, by the way." Leopold handed Timmy an envelope. The mailing address was in gold cursive, with a subtle crimson outline around each letter. The envelope opened upon Timmy's touch, revealing a suicide king playing card. Timmy picked up the card, flipped it. The back was black, smooth. Gold cursive appeared on the open envelope.

Only one will be allowed to leave this table.

The envelope folded back to the way it was, lighting itself on fire. Timmy ran to where he kept the fire extinguisher. The envelope left no trace on its existence on his desk.

"What…just happened?" Timmy doesn't see Leopold's jaw hanging.

"I…don't know."

* * *

"He was selected. The card came in the mail just like

you thought it would."

"Excellent, Peter, excellent. I couldn't have set this up better. Do we have any idea who the other players will be yet?"

"I don't. Something about the cards makes whoever receives them invisible to me, except for Timmy."

"Very well then. Go check on the boy. We only need him for a few more days."

* * *

The camera lens cracked as Timmy tried taking a photo of the playing card. He caught his reflection on its midnight black surface.

"Darn. Something about this card…it refuses to let me take its picture."

"How…do you figure?"

"You did just see what I just saw right, when the envelope set itself on fire but didn't burn the desk at all?" Leopold nodded. "It doesn't take a boy detective to figure out we're dealing with something incredibly strange and powerful."

"You could…refuse to play."

"I don't think that's what my father has planned. Why didn't he tell me about…" Timmy trailed off, his right arm helping feed fingernails between his teeth. Once he looked down, he cinched his wrist and took the cuticle buffet away. "Leo, I'm gonna need you to do me a favor."

"What's that?"

* * *

The water in the basin lapped at Timmy's feet. Leopold cut the cord from the lamp, exposing the live split ends.

"Are you sure…this is…the right way?"

"This is the only way, Leo. This is the fastest way that I can get his attention. Him and I need to have a conversation."

Leopold's body froze. The water held still. From Leopold mouth came the words, "You've come so far so fast, my son. You have much further to go."

"Why did you do this, Father?"

"Tsk. Tsk. You didn't question me back then. Why question me now? Faith, boy, have it and eventually everything will make sense. You have the card and you've figured out what those five dead boys all had in common. You'll have to figure out how they're all connected."

"Couldn't you let me talk to the boys before you process them?"

"They aren't here."

"So am I here to figure out how or why we keep losing souls?"

"Don't worry yourself about that. Now sleep." Timmy's head dropped, a snore oozing out of his nose. Leopold blinked, feeling his arms and legs return to him. "How could you let him do that?"

"What…choice did I have?"

"You could have talked him out of it. What kind of guardian are you, Leopold? It would be very easy for me to put you back where I rescued you from. Make sure you keep him on task. Your reward will be great if you do. Your punishment will be greater if you don't."

Chapter 3

1.

The stack of poker chips sits in the middle of the table. John peers over his cards at the hooded figure sitting across from him. John places two cards face down on the table. The hooded figure picks up the deck and deals John two cards. The hooded figure places one card face down and deals himself one card.

"I like my chances, mystery man. I'm likin' my chances quite a bit."

"John, I don't think you understand the rules here."

"What are you talkin' about?"

"No bluffing works in this game. You should know that by now." The hooded figure moves his left arm around. John looks at the four statues sitting at the table. "We must show our cards. Whoever has the best hand, wins this game. Talking like that didn't help you before and it won't help you now. Call."

John places his cards on the table. Three 7s (♥, ♦, ♠), Ace high (♥). The hooded figure puts down two pair—5s (♥, ♣) and 9s (♦, ♣).

"Holy shit! Holy shit, I won! I fuckin' won! Woohoo!" John steps away from the table, walking around. "I told you I had a good chance of winnin'" He nearly shoves his index finger at the hooded figure. The hooded man grabs John's index finger.

"No need to gloat." The hooded man's hand glows red. John winces and drops to his knees until the hooded man lets go. "You may have won, but I do not have to tolerate your poor sportsmanship, understand?" John nods. "Good. As per the rules, you may make one request and I must grant it."

"I want my crimes erased—that man I killed, the family I burned to death—I want it all forgotten. When I walk out of this buildin', John Grant will be a free man. Can you do that? Do you think you can do that?"

"You want your crimes erased and forgotten, is that right? You want to be free, is that right? Is this what you want, John?"

"That's right. That's what I want. I want to walk out of here cleared of my crimes a free fuckin' man."

The hooded figure gets up, stands over the poker table. "As you wish, John." He raises his arms in the air. "Oh, powers of Chaos, grant John Grant the erasure of his crimes and his freedom on this plane of existence. I give you these four men in tribute for this favor. May the power of our hands guide yours." The building rumbles. The four statues glow, various shades of red light bleed onto the table, into the ground. The statues fall out of their seats, reverting to the bodies they once were. A column of red energy bursts from the table, leaving a hole in the ceiling, what's left on fire. Everything stops. The hooded man slumps in his chair. "It is done, Mr. Grant. It is done. I suggest you leave this place before the entire town burns to the ground." The hooded man disappears.

"What's goin' on in here?" The sheriff walks in, gun drawn. "Put your fuckin' hands up."

"Just a poker game, sheriff. Just a poker game."

"Really? I see four bodies and the roof's on fire. Tryin' to burn the evidence?"

"Sheriff, it's just a poker game. I didn't kill these men. The cards did. The cards."

"How did cards kill those men? I see bullet holes and blood coming out of them. I think you killed them, you son of a bitch."

John looks behind his shoulder and sees one of them on the ground, full of bullet holes, swimming in a pool of blood. "That's…"

"You're comin' with me." The sheriff walks over to John. John draws his revolver from his holster, shoots the sheriff in the knee and then in the head. A burning beam falls onto the sheriff's body, blocking the entrance.

"To Hell with you, Sheriff. I just got my freedom. There's no fuckin' way I'm losing it again."

The fire eats more of the floor and walls, growing stronger. John puts his duster over his head and jumps out of the window. He takes the burning duster off, stomps it on the ground. Several rifle hammers cock.

"Put your hands in the air." The deputy aims his rifle at John's head.

"To Hell with you all." As John pulls out both of his revolvers, the deputy and his posse open fire, punching John's body with bullets until he falls to the ground.

"That's for the Sheriff, you bastard."

"Deputy, look." One of the posse points to the window where a hooded figure climbs out. The hooded figure brushes off his knees.

"Hands in the air, motherfucker or we will shoot," the deputy yells.

"Shouldn't you worry about the fire, deputy? If you don't put it out, it'll consume the whole town."

"The Fire Brigade will take care of it."

"Don't be too sure of that." The deputy looks and watches men pass pail by pail, the water evaporating before it even touches the fire.

"What the..."

"Haven't you seen fires of Hell before, deputy?" The

hooded man claws his hands slightly and then points them at the deputy and his posse. A column of fire comes down from the roof, swallowing the men. The hooded man points his arms outward, dissipating the column, leaving charred skeletons, mixing the smell of charred flesh and gunpowder into the smoke and flame consuming the town.

"Nathaniel, where are you?" The hooded man calls out. "Nathaniel?" A man in a black hat and pinstripe suit steps out of hiding from the rock close to the bodies of the deputy and his posse.

"Here, master."

"Good. Have you made the necessary preparations?"

"Yes, master."

"This town is going to burn to the ground as an apology for my failure. The fact that he did not let me die back there means he forgives me."

"It does look like that, sir." The hooded figure sees in Nathaniel's glasses the reflection of the fire brigade struggling to stop the fire from chewing up their town. "Sir, we should go now, before we are seen. The sign is this way." Nathaniel and the hooded figure walk west.

* * *

Nathaniel and the hooded figure step over the bodies in the house. An elaborate pentagram is carved near the fireplace, with elaborate runes surrounding the outer circle. The hooded figure takes off his hood, revealing slicked back black hair, dull brown eyes, a Roman nose, and a weak jawline. He hands Nathaniel a black tin.

"Place the deck in the middle of the pentagram. We must see where we are heading next."

"Yes, Mr. Valin, I mean, sir." Nathaniel places the black tin in the middle of the pentagram and then steps back to be by Mr. Valin's side. Mr. Valin raises his arms in the air, hands glowing.

"Oh powers of Chaos, guide us in how we can best serve you. Who may we feed you to satisfy your unending desires?" The pentagram forms a column of red energy, stopping at the ceiling. Where the deck was, a black goat takes its place. Mr. Valin takes a step back. "Master?"

"I am not strong enough yet to take my full form on this plane of existence," the black goat bleats. "I'm not strong enough to leave this circle, yet. If I was, I would have bitten off your hands for failing me. Again."

"Sir, it is not my fault. He drew a better hand. Such is the will of Chaos." The black goat stares at Mr. Valin's stomach. Mr. Valin falls to the floor, doubled over in pain.

"My will is to rule this world. Your job is to unleash the apocalypse I need to regain my true form on earth to accomplish this. While you have brought me this far, I am not afraid to replace you if you continue to fail me, do you understand?" Mr. Valin nods. "Good boy. Nathaniel?"

"Yes, great one."

"Get the map. I will show you where you must go next while Mr. Valin squirms." The black goat stares at Mr. Valin's hands. They curl up into gnarled, twisted claws. "You won't need those for a bit, until you understand the price of failing me. My goodwill with you is running out. Do you understand?" Mr. Valin nods. "Good boy." Nathaniel brings the map over to the black goat. "I will send Nathaniel to the next city to begin recruiting for the next game. Once you are well, step into the circle and you will be able to follow him. The deck will stay with him until then. You need to wallow for a bit, boy. Nathaniel, come into the circle please and touch me." Nathaniel walks through the column of energy and into the middle of the circle with the black goat. He touches the goat's neck. The column tightens around them until they disappear and a thin beam of light pierces the ceiling. Mr. Valin lays on his back, sucking in air, trying to open and close his hands but can't.

* * *

"This is sure delicious," Kent says between bites of his chicken and dumplings.

"Well thank you, dear," Caroline says. A red column of energy bursts through the roof and lands in front of the fireplace. Kent gets up from the table and grabs the shotgun near the living room.

"Caroline, go get the sheriff. Now." Caroline runs to the front door. As her hand touches the knob, a knife flies out of the column, pinning her hand to the door.

When the column disappears, it reveals a man with a black hat and a pinstripe suit. He takes his watch from his vest, looks at it and presses the top. As Kent fires, two knives lodge into the barrels. Kent moans blood on the floor. The man in the pinstripe suit walks over to Kent.

"Sorry about your luck. You and your wife should be honored that you were chosen for a greater good."

* * *

Nathaniel opens the black tin and places it in the middle of the still simmering pentagram in front of the fireplace. He unsheathes two Bowie knives with obsidian blades from his inner coat pockets. Nathaniel points the knives at the blood and raises his arms. The blood rises from the floor, collecting into a ball. He conducts the blood into the tin. The red column reappears with the black goat in the middle.

"Nathaniel, you have learned so much. I love to watch you work."

Nathaniel kneels. "Thank you, master. Am I ready yet to be the new Dealer?"

"Soon. Quite soon. Your time will come. If it doesn't come soon from Benjamin failing again, it will come once you are ready to challenge him to a winner-take-all hand."

"I am tired of being submissive to that incompetent fool, master. I know I can be a far superior servant to you."

"Patience. You must let chance do its dirty work. We must trust in it. It is the most powerful force in the universe. It is the only force that can set me free. You have work to do. Let the deck guide you to the first person for the next game."

The black goat and red column disappear, leaving the uncovered black tin. Nathaniel puts the lid on the tin, holds it in his left hand, and walks out of the house.

* * *

"Nathaniel? Nathaniel, where are you?" Benjamin wanders through the middle of town, his back still smoking. He runs into a man wearing a brown bowler and sack suit.

"Are you ok?"

"Yeah…yeah I am." Benjamin looks into his eyes, his heart beating in his throat. "Um, I'm trying to find a friend and I can't seem to find him."

"Let's go have a drink and retrace your steps. I'm Henry. Henry Wormwood." He extends his right hand.

"Benjamin Valin." As Benjamin shakes Henry's hand, his heart crests, crashes against him. *Why am I feeling like this?*

2.

A pack of silver, lightning shaded coyotes burst through the clouds, rushing a man in a white suit and Stetson. He snaps the neck of the one that bites his forearms.

Rotting crimson oozes through the sleeve, drips onto the desert sand. The other coyotes circle.

"Shaman, you've ruined my suit. For that, you will pay." The white suited man raises his arms. The wind kicks the sand viciously until a sandstorm surrounds the coyotes, swallowing them one by one. When the white suited man drops his arms, the sand and wind settle, revealing an old Apache, gagging and bleeding. "You dare summon me to fight me? Me? I trade in desires, wants, things people think they need. They give me their pound of flesh willingly in exchange, like your daughter. I will take yours in retribution." A knife lands in the white suited man's left shoulder. He grips the bone handle.

"I wouldn't do that if I were you, demon," warns a thick, sultry Eastern European accent from the darkness.

"Helena, is that you? How is your father doing? Oh wait, I know how he is doing. You'll be joining him soon." The white suited man tightens his grip on the knife handle and pulls. His stomach, intestines boil as he grips and pulls harder. He coughs up black tar, curdling blood. A long haired woman emerges from the darkness.

"The blade is coated in sage. Leaving it in means you die slowly. Pulling it out means you die quickly."

"The only one dying here is you, Helena." The white suited man places his hand on the ground. His eyes roll back. The ground trembles for a moment and then nothing. "Why…" A burst of light illuminates the white suited man, Helena, and the wounded shaman.

"You have lost your connection, demon. The sage has taken care of that." A figure in a light gray cloak and hood appears next to the demon. The figure takes a black tin out of its cloak, places it next to the wounded white suited man and opens the lid.

"Wizard…oh…wizard…you cannot kill me. As long as desire and want exist, you can not…destroy me."

"Who said anything about destroying you?" The cloaked and hooded figure steps back. "Apollo, aim true with your arrows of light to hold this demon still so we may cleanse the earth of its existence." A volley of arrows made of stars pins the demon to the sand by his hands, shoulders, and legs.

"You…will not…get away with this. None of you. Mark my words. My day will come."

"Not tonight."

Helena pulls the shaman to his feet and they limp over to the wizard. They encircle the pinned demon, holding hands. The chants of Latin, Apache, and Romani harmonize. The black tin begins pulling in the demon.

"You think…you think you have won, you fools. You've won…" The black tin pulls the demon apart, sucking each piece in. Once the tin absorbs the last of the demon, the circle breaks.

"Destroy it, Lucius. Destroy it once and for all," hisses Helena. The wizard takes off his hood, revealing a gaunt face, dimly glowing brown eyes.

"The demon was right. As long as the greed of men exists, he cannot die." He points his cane at the tin. "However, the demon can be dismembered." The top of Lucius' cane glows. From the tin, a deck of poker cards levitate. The deck pulls itself apart, forming four rows of thirteen. "Swift feet of Hermes, deliver these cards into hands that cannot harm us." The cards levitate higher in the air and scatter. Lucius drops to his right knee, his cane keeping him from collapsing.

"What about the tin?" Helena asks.

"The tin is his body. The cards are his soul. As long as they are kept separate, the demon cannot reform. Even if he does, it will take a lot to bring him back to full strength and form. Helena, you must…"

The Apache howls. Eyes and teeth have the shaman by the throat. In one quick motion, the teeth swallow part of his neck. Another set of eyes and teeth grab Helena's raised left arm, ripping it off before ripping out her throat. Eight sets of eyes and teeth stalk the wizard.

"I…will…not…die. Not…like…"

3.

"Jesus fuckin' Christ. What the fuck happened here?" From his horse, Donald spits tobacco near the drying pools of blood and torn clothing.

"Sir, I have no clue." The dirty Stetson keeps the sun out of the boy's dull brown eyes, Roman nose, and weak jawline.

"Go take a look, Ben. See if you can recover anything."

"Why do I have to always do that, goddammit?"

"Because I'm your father. And you could use a little toughening. Get off your horse, boy, and see if you can find anything."

Ben slowly climbs off the horse. He walks around each pool, examining shreds of clothing with the barrel of his rifle. "There's nothing here, pa. It looks like a pack of wolves did this."

"No fuckin' way wolves did this. Coyotes maybe, but wolves? Keep lookin'." Donald takes a bottle out of his saddle bag and sips. Ben continues looking around until he sees a smooth black tin sticking out of the sand.

"Pa, I found something." He walks over to the tin and touches it.

Hello, Benjamin.

Ben jumps back from the tin. "Who said that?"

"Boy what are you doing over there?"

"Nothin'…pa." Ben touches the tin again.

Hello, Benjamin. Can you hear me?

"Who are you?" Ben whispers.

No need to whisper. Just think the words and I'll hear them.

Who are you?

Benjamin, aren't you tired of living in your father's shadow.

I don't know what you are talkin' about.

Oh I think you do. How's your eye? Ben feels his right eye throbbing from last night's elbow while trying to drag his father home from the saloon.

It's...fine. It's fine.

Aren't you tired of his incompetence? He doesn't deserve to live, don't you think? Ben lets go of the tin. *That won't work now, boy. I can taste the hatred in you. What if I told you I could help you solve your problems, to be free of your family?*

How?

I need your father's blood. Ben walks backwards, slowly at first, then faster. He turns around and runs until he hops on his horse and gallops off.

"Where the fuck are you goin' boy? I swear to fuckin' God, I'll beat you when I get my hands on you."

4.

Benjamin sits against the door, feeling the thud of his father's boot tip through the wood.

It would be easy to kill him when he sleeps, Benjamin. A knife to the throat. A rock to his head.

"You better let me in you little fuck! I might not kill you if you do."

"I want ma back. I want her back so bad." Benjamin squeezes his eyes, trying to dam his tears. He dives into his shirt sleeve.

"I'll give you somethin' to fuckin' cry about." Benjamin feels the boot heel and wood dig into his shoulder, then nothing. He heaves, pursing his dry lips. The door knob explodes, punching a pillow on his bed. Benjamin tries scurrying under his bed. His ankle wants to collapse in his father's grip. He almost grows splinters for chest hair.

5.

How are you, Benjamin?

You know how I am. The tingle of his father's fingers loosen around his neck. He winces with each swallow.

You can stop this. I can help you.

Can you bring my ma back? That's the only way he'll stop being like this.

I can. I just need your father's blood.

I don't want to kill him.

Silly boy, you can get his blood without killing him. Help me, and I will help you get what you need. Place a small bit of your hair in the tin if we have a deal.

You can really bring ma back?

I can but not without your help. If your father keeps this up, you will die. That shotgun almost clipped you earlier. If he was any drunker, we wouldn't be talking. Do we have a deal?

Benjamin pinches a strand of hair, yanks it and places it in the tin. His stomach sours for a moment. The tingle around his neck disappears. He still winces with every swallow. *It's the best I can do, for now. Can you walk?* Benjamin nods. *Good. Go into the bathroom and touch the strop.*

The what?

The thing he uses to sharpen the razor he shaves with.

Oh.

Go.

Benjamin twists, legs dangling from the bed. He places his left foot on the floor, cautiously, then his right. The bed yawns when he stands. Benjamin waits for his father's whiskeyed yowl. The balls of his feet dodge each creak until he stands in the kitchen, facing the strop.

Closer, boy. Closer. I just need for you to touch it with your left hand. Benjamin shuffles closer until he can stretch the strop taut. His fingers glow red, then black, feeding it to the strop. His right hand clutches his stomach.

Almost, boy. Almost. You are doing good. The light climbs back into Benjamin's fingers. He almost drops to his knees until lightning wraps around his spine. *Can't have you fall now or else he'll wake up.*

What have you done?

Shhhh. No questions. We have a deal, remember? Now, sleep. Benjamin's eyes roll back, sealed behind lead eyelids. He shambles back to his bedroom and flops down, gently.

6.

Donald whets the blade on the strop. The edge presses against his right cheek. Something bites the nerves in his hand.

7.

Benjamin lumbers out of bed toward the bathroom, the black tin in his left hand. He stands in the door frame, looking at the deep cut in Donald's neck, the blood all over the floor and slightly on the wall. Benjamin takes the lid off the tin and places it next to Donald's body. He points his arms at the blood, spreading his fingers wide. A decaying red light engulfs Benjamin's fingers. The blood begins lifting from the ground, peeling from the wall, each drop adding to the sphere above Donald's body. Benjamin moves his arms slowly, the sphere moving with them until it hovers above the black tin. He points his fingers slightly down. The sphere slowly bleeds into the black tin. The blood seeps into the tin, settling between the sides. Benjamin seals the tin. His eyelids open.

"What…what have you done?" Benjamin's right hand covers his mouth.

I did nothing. It was just an accident.

"Yes you did. Whatever you did to his…strop…did this to him, I know this." A fire grows in Benjamin's stomach.

Boy, we had a deal. You wanted your mother back and

in order for me to start the process, I needed your father's blood. You agreed to help me. I have no control over what your father did, the clumsy fool.

"I think…you…I think you did have some control." Molten lava snakes through Benjamin's intestines.

I'm not afraid to kill you, boy. It would be the fastest way to see your mother though, wouldn't it? Benjamin feels his kidneys boil.

"No…no…I'm sorry. I'm sorry. A deal…is a deal." The burning and boiling simmer, then stop. Benjamin writhes and gasps on the floor.

Good boy. Good boy. Once you're ready, take the tin into the kitchen. We have work to do.

8.

Benjamin removes the knife from his father's belt. He picks up the tin and walks into the kitchen, placing it on the table.

Benjamin, I'm going to show you a diagram. You'll take the knife and I'll guide your hand. Understand? Benjamin points the knife downward and gets on his knees. He furiously carves an intricate circle with various symbols holding together the crooked pentagram. Benjamin stands, the knife tumbles out of his throbbing hand.

That…that will have to do. Place me in the the center and then step away far outside of the circle. Benjamin takes the tin from the table, places it in the center of the pentagram. Red decaying light grows from the tin, pouring slowly into the pentagram, the outer circle holding it together. Benjamin covers his eyes with his right forearm. The red decaying light chokes the room. The tin crumples. Something tries to punch its way out from the inside but the tin holds. It levitates, the metal oscillating and twisting furiously. When it stops, a fly hovers.

"This is worse than I thought…much much worse." The fly's voice clangs throughout the room. Benjamin walks closer to the fly. "Stop, boy. You cannot come in here. Not now."

"What are you?"

"I was once…a man…kind of a man…but a man. That damn wizard, what did he do? What did he do? Benjamin, do you remember where you found the tin?" Benjamin shakes his head. "Approach the circle, boy." Benjamin creeps toward the circle, stopping at the edge. "Place your hand through the circle." A decaying red energy barrier appears, parting just enough to let Benjamin's hand through. The barrier holds his arm still as the fly lands on his finger. Benjamin jerks and twitches, blood trickles out of his nose, on his lips. The barrier lets him go, the floor knocking the air, his consciousness out.

9.

Awake yet, boy?

Benjamin counts the cracks in the wooden ceiling. He

rolls over to his left and notices the black tin sitting on the floor closed, the circle sizzling. *What did you do?*

Never mind that, boy. Your father took from the desert a cane with a silver top and tip. He locked it in the chest at the foot of the bed. I need you to retrieve it.

Benjamin rolls on his stomach, pushes himself up onto his knees and shins, slowly making his way upright. *Look, you keep hurtin' me and givin' me nothin' back in return. Am I your partner or your puppet?*

Both. Benjamin's legs stiffen. He clomps from the kitchen into his father's bedroom, stopping in front of the oak steamer chest at the foot of the bed. Benjamin fights his arm, index finger from extending. The lock pops and falls with a dull thud. Lightning bursts through the lid and into Benjamin. His body slides across the floor, sizzling.

"Using a child for a conduit? You must be desperate, demon." A figure in a gray cloak and hood appears in front of the open chest. It walks closer to Benjamin, pointing his cane. Benjamin's eyes blacken, straining his neck to look directly at the figure.

"I wondered who summoned the wolves, wizard, and I knew it couldn't have been me since I was so weak." The words come out of Benjamin's mouth like boiled whiskey and smoke. "Why did you do it?"

"The others...they wanted to dispel you forever. It could have been done, but I have plans to harness your power." The wizard points his cane to the roof.

A lightning bolt makes a hole over Benjamin's body. "Apollo, aim true with your arrows of light to hold this demon still so I may cleanse the earth of its existence." The sky stays overcast. "Apollo, aim true with your arrows of light to hold this demon still so I may cleanse the earth of its existence." A herd of clouds continues rumbling forward.

"It looks like you lost your connection to who you call The One, wizard." Benjamin's body pulls itself up slowly. "When you invoked the wolves and betrayed your friends, he cut you off, like your friends cut me off."

"Don't you make another move, demon." The wizard points his cane at Benjamin's body. "I am not afraid to kill your conduit." Benjamin's body keeps one knee and hand on the ground. Red, decaying light spills from his fingers to beneath where the wizard stands. The wood gives underneath the wizard's weight. His howl muffles the snapping of both of his ankles. Benjamin's body stands and walks towards the upper half of the wizard. He bends down to look into the wizard's eyes.

"Tell me what I need to know, wizard, and I may let you live."

"I'll...tell you nothing."

Benjamin's body takes the hood off the wizard and puts his hands on wizard's temples and cheeks. "You will tell me everything."

10.

Wake up.

The decaying smile on the wizard's neck greets Benjamin. He skitters backward, slamming against the far wall of the kitchen. "What did you do?"

Saved your life, boy. That cane your father took...the wizard who owned it...he used it as a homing beacon of some kind. That's some of what I got out of him. Some.

"He called you 'demon'. Why?"

Why do you keep talking out loud? You can just think the words and I'll hear you.

"Because it sounds weird, thinking instead of saying. Why did he call you 'demon'?"

You don't need to know, boy.

Benjamin squeezes his eyes.

You don't. Need. To know. Boy. Benjamin feels his intestines twist around a fiery set of hands. Benjamin squeezes his eyes, grits his teeth. His intestines knot tighter, burn. Benjamin inches his way on his belly toward his father's knife laying next to the wizard's body.

What are you doing? Benjamin's fingers reach for the handle.

"You...won't...kill me. You...need...me...too... like...I...need...you." Benjamin's hand tightens around the knife. "Like...you...said...I...can...join...my... family...faster...this...way." Benjamin turns on his back. He points the knife downward and thrusts. The tip stops half an inch from Benjamin's bare, pale stomach.

You're right. I need you. Benjamin's intestines untie and cool down. The knife falls, sticks into the floor. *I will show you what you need to know. Open your mind.*

Chapter 4

1.

Len Soriano sat in the easy chair in his hotel room, looking at his glass of scotch. He almost let some of it fall out of his mouth when he heard the three steady knocks at the door. He walked over to the door and peered out the peephole. Len only saw the top of the person's New York Mets baseball cap.

"What's the password," Len asked.

"Video poker…is for fags."

Len turned the lock and let his dealer into the hotel room. "What took you so long, man? Did you bring the vitamin M?" Len noticed when his dealer finally looked up that he had a salt and pepper handlebar mustache. "Wait a minute, you're not…" Len didn't have enough time to register the crack to the bridge of his nose, the first and only incision to his throat. The dealer ran into the bathroom, threw up in the toilet, and washed the blood out of his hands.

"It's…done," the dealer said to the running water. "It's…done."

"Very good. You did well. As long as you continue doing as I say, no one will ever find out about this."

2.

"Wh…where…where am I?"

"That was quite the nasty spill you took in your hotel room. You lost a lot of blood. For a moment, I thought we were going to lose you, too."

"Wha…what are you talking about? Who are you?"

"I'm Doctor David Samson, Mr. Soriano. I'll be overseeing your care while you're here."

"Where's…here?"

"St. Malverde's Hospital, Mr. Soriano. Housekeeping found you passed out, almost dog paddling in a mixture of blood and scotch. It was a strange scene they said, you in a five star hotel drinking a brand not even fit for a plastic bottle."

"Well doc…in my line of work…you have to know what to take a chance on, and be careful how you spend your money. A good hotel will always beat booze."

"And methamphetamine?"

"Huh?"

"Mr. Soriano, I'm not an idiot. The only way someone would pass out as hard as you did would be by drinking cheap scotch and smoking methamphetamine. I'm not sure which is chemically better for you, probably the scotch, but not by much."

"Vitamin M…helps me keep sharp, Doc, especially for those grueling 30 hour sits at the table."

"Prolonged use of what you call 'Vitamin M' will kill you. Based on the color of your teeth, you won't have them much longer if you keep this up."

"Spare me the lecture, doc. When can I get out of here?"

"A few days. We need to keep you here under observation, run some tests. Your liver isn't looking so good, Mr. Soriano. We need to see if it is still functioning and if not, we'll have to discuss next steps."

"But, the tournament…"

"The tournament can wait, Mr. Soriano. Your body can't. I suggest you rest."

"Goddamn…fine, fine. Run your damn tests. I'm going to lose so much money from this, I hope you know that, Doc."

"Would you rather lose your money or your life, Mr. Soriano?"

3.

"Did he buy it, Peter?"

"He did. Mr. Soriano doesn't remember a thing about how he really got here."

"Excellent, excellent. We just need to keep him distracted for a few days."

"Can you keep this up, between the boy and him?"

"Something will give."

"I understand your concern, Gatekeeper, and I've planned for this. What's the political stability looking like in Libya?"

"According to our operatives, shaky at best."

"Good, very good. Tell our operatives to get the ball rolling down there. Who we receive up here will help keep things going."

"Do I go as something powerful and awe inspiring or be a bit more subtle?"

"Subtle. We don't have the kind of bandwidth to pull that off right now. We have to keep Mr. Soriano and the boy detective thinking they're in the hospital only for a few more days. Mr. Soriano makes for an excellent insurance policy in order for us to succeed, especially once the game begins in three days. We will be forever grateful for Mr. Soriano's unknowing sacrifice when all goes according to my plan."

"You mean if."

"No, Peter, when. It's times like this that I'm glad I have so much faith in me."

4.

Timmy sat at the lunch table, studying the guide on Texas Hold 'em.

"Mind if I sit here?" Carlos Francisco loomed over Timmy, his faded black trenchcoat hiding part of his Metallica *Master of Puppets* t-shirt.

"Um…I'm actually kind of busy here. Can this wait?"

"What are you so busy with, buddy?"

"We're…we're not buddies. In fact, we've never spoken until yesterday, but you know that already, don't you?"

"Yeah, Timmy never even suspected me in any of his cases, that was one thing I was impressed about him. He was a true detective."

"I'm still here, Carlos."

"Timmy's body perhaps, but not…his *soul*. I guess would be the right word, soul. You aren't Timmy. You might walk and talk like him but you aren't him. Guess we'll find out for sure soon enough."

Timmy closed his book, folded his hands over it. "What?"

"This." Carlos reached inside his trenchcoat, pulling out a one-eyed Jack poker card, then flipping it to the other side to show Timmy the glossy black back. "I got this two days ago. I have a feeling you did, too."

"I don't know what you're talking about."

"Timmy's never been into games like poker. He's more

of the goal oriented, activity type—like martial arts or detective work. There's an objective, and he always achieves it. Always. The thing about being an outcast is you get really good at watching those around you. And making fun of them quietly, but mostly watching."

"Well, Carlos, have you considered that I'm still wrapping my head around the death of my parents or the fact that a week ago, I woke up from a coma? Or that this could be part of a case I'm working on to take my mind off of all this shit?"

"Wow…Timmy Hightower actually saying a curse word. Now I know you aren't him. He'd never lose his cool like this."

"How would you feel if both of your parents died suddenly?"

Carlos turned sharply, his trenchcoat bobbing with each step. "I'll see you in two days, not Timmy," he said over his shoulders.

* * *

Timmy sat in the chair facing Chief Donaldson's desk, puffing away at his pipe. "How is going with the case, Timmy?"

"I think I might have a break in the case. I actually need some information that's related to it."

"Anything, Timmy, anything."

"What do you know about Carlos Francisco?"

"Are you…are you sure you want to know?"

"Chief, how bad can it be?"

"Once you see the case file on his parents, you'll understand."

5.

"Peter, why can't I find anything on Carlos Francisco."

"Did you talk to his parents?"

"I already thought of that."

"And…"

"They never made it here."

"Could it be they were atheists or agnostics?"

"Possibly. I hate that I don't know. I'm supposed to be all knowing, at least among those who believe. Carlos somehow knows that Timmy Hightower isn't Timmy Hightower and I need to make sure he stays quiet."

"How will you do that?"

* * *

The tip of the throwing knife teased Carlos Francisco's throat while the other hand firmly held Carlos up against the metal double sliding doors of his closet.

"You…will leave Timmy Hightower alone… understood?"

The playing card levitated out of the left inner pocket of Carlos's trenchcoat. Carlos watched the Jack's one eye glow over the gloved hand on his throat.

"What...are you...looking at?"

Carlos and Leopold collapsed. The playing card stayed afloat, starting at both of them with its one eye.

"So...Timmy sent you...to scare me, huh?" Carlos coughed out the question. "The throwing knife...to the throat was a dead giveaway, Mr. Franz." The man writhed beneath the light of the Jack's one eye. "I'm sure the police would love a second chance at finally catching you."

Carlos brought himself upright, then walked over to his nightstand. A throwing knife took the cellphone out of Carlos's hand, pinning it on the wall. The next one cut the landline to the phone on Carlos's desk. The butt of the third knife knocked Carlos out, the playing card falling to the floor at the same time.

* * *

"What happened in there?" The running water in the bathroom sink asked Leopold.

"What do you mean...what happened in there. You... didn't see what happened in there?"

"I saw everything and then I couldn't see anything at all for a couple of minutes until you left Carlos's house."

"Shit...I left my knives behind. I...didn't have time to collect them, with everything that happened."

"What happened?"

"Carlos...received the same type of playing card... Timmy received. When I did...as you asked, the playing card...floated...and did something to me that made me drop the knife and the boy. Whatever strength you gave me...I had to use to destroy his cellphone, cut his landline, and knock the boy out. I was able to leave once the card stopped doing whatever it was doing. I thought you were all knowing, all seeing."

"Are you questioning my power, Leopold? I've been able to protect you thus far. It if it wasn't for me, you'd still be in prison."

"I'm sorry...I'm just shaken up. What about the knives? The boy figured out...it was me."

"Leave the knives and the boy to me."

The water stopped running. Leopold cupped some of the water, splashing it on his face. "I hope you know what you're doing."

6.

"You can't go in there. Stop!" The diving suit clanged past Dr. Samson toward the door leading to the ICU. Dr. Samson extended his right arm, opening his hand. "Stop!" The diving suit bowed slightly backward, its arms and legs trying to push forward.

"I...want...to...see...my...parents."

Dr. Samson's right arm shook as the diving suit pulled away from the invisible tether trying to wrap itself around its back and arms. "Stop! Stop! You know...not what you do, Tim." The diving suit stopped, turned.

"Dr. Samson…Dr. Samson never, ever called me, Tim. Who are you? And where am I?"

"He's figured it out. Can we finally tell him?"

"Who are you talking to?"

"It's time. No need to keep up this charade, Peter."

The diving suit's neck creaked craning around the room. "Who said that?"

"Alright." Peter waved his right arm, the off-white walls, sterile tiles disintegrating, revealing a stark white room. A snap of his fingers skinned Dr. Samson off of Peter's frame. "Timmy…I'm sorry that we had to lie to you but it was the only way."

"What?"

Peter placed his palm up, a mirror materializing in it. "Here. Take a look." Timmy took the mirror from Peter's palm and noticed the brass grate surrounding the face plate of his diving suit. "The accident…the accident killed you, your mother, and father. You're…"

"If I'm where you're about to say I am, then where's my mom and dad? They should be here with me too."

"Well…that's the thing, Timmy. Your parents aren't here. We're working on trying to find out why."

"Who…who is we?"

"Me. And him. And his son. We had to keep you in the suit in order to have a bridge to place him in your body. He's the only one that can figure out where your parents are or why they aren't here."

"Wait a minute. Doesn't…"

"Don't say his name. He hates being called that."

"Doesn't…he…see everything?"

"Not this, Timmy. Not this. Believe me, we don't normally do this. We'd let you go in peace but we have to stop this happening again."

"I could solve this myself, y'know. If you let me go back, I could do this. I've solved a lot of cases. I could solve this one too."

"This sort of thing cannot be perceived by human eyes or hearts, Timmy, or else we would send you back. You're in the suit because that grants him access to your skills, talents, your memories so he can blend in, so he can track down the cause of your parents' missing souls, find them, and stop it from ever happening again. If he is successful, if you are patient a little longer, we'll reward you and your parents."

"How?"

"We can make the accident never happen. You'll have your life, their lives back."

"Won't that undo finding out how my parents souls disappeared, though?"

"He wrote the rules of time and space. He can edit them at will."

"I'll do anything to get my parents back. We have a deal, Peter."

* * *

"Did he buy it?"

"Yeah…yeah he did. He's all in, now. That should make things easier for him down there."

"Excellent…the back up plan worked then. I knew it was a matter of time that the boy detective would figure things out, being a boy detective and all."

"What now?"

"I need you to clean up a mess."

"Leopold?"

"Yes. We still need him for a little longer. We can't have anything get back to him."

"How do you want me to do it?"

"It's up to you."

7.

"When 'Princes of the Universe' played loudly, I knew what they were doing in there. No matter how loud they turned up the music, I could hear their screams. It wasn't like the kind of screaming that was all sexy, like on Cinemax or HBO late Friday night. Their blood trailed behind them when they walked out of the bedroom. They always tried hiding it behind their bathrobes but some of it always soaked through, looking like really clumsy commandos."

"Do you know…do you know why they kept doing

that?"

"I...I...no...no I don't. I mean do you ask your parents what weird shit they're into when it comes to them fucking? Do you?"

"I'm sorry, I shouldn't have asked. I'm just trying to wrap my head around...around this."

"You're a really shitty cop, Chief. Got more questions for me or what? I just want to be done with this shit."

"I do, Carlos. Just one more question. How did you know to go in the room?"

"I came home from school and that song was playing so I knew to stay away from the bedroom. When it kept repeating for an hour straight, I went to the mall, dicked around Finite Jest for a while, and then came home around eight, that song still playing. There was no way that they could have been going at it that long, never have, so I went to the bedroom door and knocked. I didn't notice the squishing sound until after I opened the door and found them, wallowing in each others blood, the katanas they got when they went to Japan for their honeymoon found on opposite sides of the bed. I got the Hell out of there and called you."

The remote fell out of Timmy's hand, landing perfectly on the power button to shut off the TV.

"Do you believe me now?" Chief Donaldson huffed on his pipe.

"This...this fits...this fits the pattern. Chief, I need you to find out what other 12-13 year old boys have lost one or both parents recently, in this town and nearby towns. I need that information by tomorrow morning if we're to figure out where this could happen again."

"What do you mean 'where this could happen again'?"

Timmy took the black playing card out of the left breast pocket of his red and yellow plaid short sleeved shirt. "Carlos and I both received this, but with different suits. What happened to Larry and those four boys had something to do with these cards."

"Have you figured out what happened yet?"

"A game. A very deadly game."

* * *

"The boy is talking to the police."

"That's…unexpected. I mean it's not like they can do anything about stopping the game. The cards always protect their players until it's time."

"This could bring us the wrong kind of attention though. We're always exhausted after the game is done. At our greatest moment of weakness, we could be captured or even worse. We've survived for over a century by being subtle and cunning, hiding and waiting until it was just right to start the next game. You've gotten greedy and it will put us both at risk."

"Nathaniel, I know what I'm doing. Don't start questioning me now. The purity and nobility in that boy's soul will be just what we need if the cards are right. It's a chance worth taking."

"What…what if we lose?" Nathaniel's throat sealed itself shut.

"That's enough from you."

8.

Timmy stared at the map on the computer monitor, Leopold looking over his shoulder. "Based on the last game, the five players came from these areas." Timmy pressed a key and five red dots showed up on the map of the town representing where each boy resided. "The dots when connected make a nice pentagon but the location of the actual game was Larry's house, which you'd think should be in the center of the pentagon, not one of the points. Here's where Carlos and I are in town." Timmy pressed another key and two dots appeared representing where he and Carlos lived. "This makes a pretty good side of a pentagon. Once the Chief gets back with what I asked him for, I'll know who is most likely in the game the day after tomorrow."

"When…do you think the game will start?"

"The game Larry was in started after school but before his father could make it home from work, a nice two hour window that allowed Larry and the other boys to play without being interrupted. My best guess is that it will be around the same time, where it won't be questioned why we aren't home right after school. Most likely though, it won't be here since you'll be home."

"I…I don't have to be home. I…could be close by…

but…I don't have to be here. It might…give us the best chance…that our house hosts…the game."

Timmy stroked his chin for a moment, then swiveled the office chair to face Leopold. "That's…that's a brilliant idea, Leo. I'm going to have the Chief arrange the police to watch the other houses for suspicious activity. I'll request from Chief Donaldson that you participate in watching over our house."

"Do I…have to work with him?"

"I'm a potential victim. You have to work with the Chief."

"But…he's such…a prick."

"I can tell but if my dad said it was your duty to protect me, then you have to follow his orders, no matter if you like how you have to carry out those orders. I know my dad. If you don't do as he says, he's incredibly vengeful. Until I came along, he actually made bets with other angels to see whether he could break mankind's belief in him. Seriously, what he did to Job only captured half of what he actually did. Three words: sodomy by sandstorm. Then there was that woman who was turned into salt because her husband didn't follow my father's orders."

"I…understand. More than you know, Timmy, I understand the way your father works. For you and for him, I will stomach dealing with the police and Chief Donaldson to protect you. Speaking of protecting you… it's an hour past your bedtime."

"But Leo…"

"But…nothing."

Chapter 5

1.

"Is the receptacle ready for our 'patient', Peter?"

"Yes. I followed all of your specifications, tested it a few times just to make sure it worked."

"Good. Pull the plug quickly and have it delivered to Leopold before sunrise. My son will need all the help he can get."

"What…what if the receptacle leaks and he loses control? We've never done this before, two souls in the same body."

"We haven't tried before, Peter, that is true, but I know that it works for sure. Do you remember the burly Greek with the limp so bad he walked with a cane?"

"Well…no, I can't say that I do."

"I forget sometimes you haven't been around as long as I have. In exchange for helping him solve an interesting problem, he showed me how one body can share two souls, even how that extra soul can take control of it with the right receptacle."

*   *   *

Leopold crept into Timmy's room, his snore covering the creaks coming up from the floor every once in awhile from beneath Leopold's feet. He took Timmy's right arm into his hand and slid a bronze bracelet onto Timmy's hand until it settled on his wrist. Leopold passed his hand over the bracelet and it blended in with Timmy's fading tan. "It's done," Leopold whispered to the lazily spinning ceiling fan.

*   *   *

"Did you...sleep well, Timmy?" Leopold asked, while holding a tray with two buttered pieces of toast and a tall glass of orange juice toward Timmy as he sat in his desk chair. Timmy took the tray and placed it next to his computer.

"Yes, strangely. I should be nervous but...I don't feel nervous. I'm confident that everything will go according to plan." Timmy took a piece of toast off the tray and snapped a corner into his mouth. "This body is always so hungry."

"Eat slowly. You don't...want to cramp up. Where do you think the game...will be?"

"At one of these houses, most likely." Timmy pressed a button on his keyboard and it revealed five red dots on the map of the city. "Based on my research, each of these boys has lost one or both parents lately. It is my theory that they will also be participants in today's game, thus the game will have to be in one of those five houses. I asked the chief to have units staking out those houses, including ours, to see which house myself and the others playing today's game will be in. This will allow the police to try and stop the game even before it begins."

"I don't think...Chief Donaldson...is brave enough to try such a thing. I've been very up close and personal with his character."

"Timmy had to have thought the world of him in order to trust him unquestionably. He's saved Timmy a few times from some hairy situations, especially in 'The Case of the Shadow Student Government'."

"The chief...placed him in those hairy situations, like the one...he's placed you in now. I questioned the sanity...of your parents...and whether they were good parents. If you were mine...I wouldn't have placed you in such danger or allowed you...to be in such danger consistently."

"Timmy's parents were good parents. They let the boy make his own decisions. When I was his age in my day, 12 was like being 25. We were in constant danger. If you looked at a Roman the wrong way, your head could be on a pike by sundown. What Timmy has gone through was his choice."

"I wish...I could say the same." Leopold looked over Timmy's shoulder at the clock on the wall. "You better finish eating. If you don't leave in the next five minutes...

you'll be late for school. And…don't bother asking if you have to. You…are still in his body."

"I wasn't." Timmy gulped down his orange juice before grabbing his backpack and running up the stairs. He stopped at the door and faced Leopold. "We'll crack this case, won't we Leopold?"

"We…have to…if you want to go home."

2.

The chalkboard squealed as Ms. Ewing wrote today's pop quiz questions for her third period American History class. "Remember, spelling counts. You get no credit for the question if you misspell your answers."

"Ms. Ewing…" Timmy raised his hand, then put it away. "Never mind. Sorry."

The cursive from the chalk slowed to a clotting bleed. The lights flickered, Timmy's classmates blurred, their clothing and skin, their desks, oozing to the floor. Timmy tried to stand up but his shoulders and neck weighed like anvils.

* * *

"This is not good."

"Peter, what are you talking about?"

"Your son…I can't find him. One moment, I knew where he was and the next moment he…just vanished."

"Excellent. This means the game has started, sooner

than I anticipated, but it has begun. Alert our operative."

* * *

"It's been a long time, hasn't it, Leopold." Chief Donaldson muttered from the corner of his mouth as he puffed his pipe. "Not used to sitting in the front seat of a police car, are you?"

"Could you…open the window? I don't appreciate you…gagging me with your shitty tobacco."

"Fine, fine." Chief Donaldson pressed the switch in the door to lower the window. "Anything to get you to shut up." He looked over at the driveway and noticed the cobalt blue El Camino. "I see you've taken good care of her. It was the hardest thing I did, having to give her up, but it was necessary."

"Give…give her up?"

"Leopold, I knew you took it after you were acquitted. Hell, I left the keys in the ignition, left it running while I was in the MiniMart getting some beer. I knew you wouldn't kill me. Would have been too obvious and your ass would have been back in front of a judge faster than your head could spin. I figured you learned your lesson about letting revenge cloud your judgment and would take advantage of the situation."

A dove landed on the hood of Chief Donaldson's squad car, pecked a little at the windshield and stared at Chief Donaldson. "Hmmm. You sure?" The dove pecked at the windshield again and nodded. "You got it."

"Got...what?" Leopold caught in the corner of his eye Chief Donaldson clumsily reaching for the yellow and black Taser holstered on his belt. The first punch broke Chief Donaldson's nose. Leopold pulled one of his knives out of his vest, held it to Chief Donaldson's throat. "That...was stupid, Craig. Really...stupid. I think it's time...we had a talk." Leopold blocked Chief Donaldson's attempt at a right cross, teased the blade against his neck. In one fluid motion, Leopold pulled another knife from his vest and severed the cord tethering the radio to the receiver. "No backup...no assistance... no help. We...talk, just you...and me."

"I...could use...a little help here." The dove flew into the car and into Leopold's face. Leopold let go of Chief Donaldson, throwing the knife that was at his throat at the dove. The lightning grew from the pit of Leopold's stomach, wrapping around his arms and legs, making him twitch and writhe in his seat. Chief Donaldson got out of the squad car, pulled Leopold outside and kneeled on his back while cuffing him. Chief Donaldson took his knee off his back, hit Leopold with a hand held Taser and sprayed his eyes with pepper spray before walking back to the squad car. "That should keep him out for awhile," Chief Donaldson said to the dove. "Thanks for the assist."

* * *

"Where...where am I?"

"Hello, 'Timmy'."

Timmy's eyes focused on Carlos Francisco's dull brown eyes, the crop of acne on his left cheek waited for harvest. "Oh shit, it's you."

"Shit? Shit? The clean cut boy detective just swears all the time now? I'm...shocked. Attempting to act more human makes you sound less human though, 'Timmy'. Do you remember the last time you were a person?"

"A moment ago in American History. How did we..." The black poker card floated out of the right pocket of Timmy's buttoned up short sleeved crisp baby blue shirt and into the open black tin in the middle of the round table. "The game though...I don't understand. Why are we starting so early?"

"So early?"

"Yeah, Carlos. The last game began after school ended and before six, that perfect gap in time for latch-key kids to do what they want without parental interference. This...it's..."

"I think it was ten or so when I woke up here."

"That would mean...about the middle of second period, the beginning of third. This is either bold or desperate."

A third boy materialized in the chair across from Carlos and Timmy. The faded neon green Polo clung to his pony keg gut. The black poker card floated from the boy's pre-torn and worn jeans back into the black tin.

"Carlos, meet Johnny Decarn. His mother and father were killed a month ago during a carjacking. The gang that killed them made Johnny watch."

"Pffff…that's fuckin' nothin'. Nothin' compared to the crazy shit I had to deal with regarding my mom and dad but you probably know that already."

"Your parents chose to do what they did. Two grown ups engaging in some seriously dangerous sex play. They at least warned you when they were doing it. Johnny wasn't given that choice to look away."

"Fuck you, 'Timmy'."

"Where…where am I?" Johnny lifted his head to look at Carlos and Timmy. "Who are you?" The cards lifted from the tin, shuffled themselves and dealt Carlos, Timmy, and Johnny two cards facedown.

"Place your bets," the tin hissed. Three large stacks of chips appeared in front of the boys, Timmy's whiskey brown, Carlos's stack ash gray, Johnny's souring blue.

"This isn't right." Timmy said. "This isn't right at all. There should be five of us playing."

"But there is." Footsteps echoed through the room. Timmy, Johnny, and Carlos turned. Standing away from the table, the man in a white suit grinned, peering at the boys slightly over a pair of gold rimmed glasses. "When the cards searched for the next players, two of them came back. They wouldn't do that unless we had five players ready to go. I can't quite figure it out now, but I'm sure I will as this game goes on. Timmy, based on what we were able to see, it looks like you've got things figured out. Care to explain to your new friends the rules of this game?"

"If my research is correct, these chips represent our souls. We play until only one of us is left standing. The last boy standing plays him." Timmy pointed at the white suited man.

"Please, call me Nate."

"If the last boy standing wins, then Nate here has to grant one wish from the winner. If Nate wins, the last boy joins the others, feeding his master over there." Timmy pointed to the tin. "The cards reward the winner or winners of each hand and punish the losers."

"I'm quite impressed, Timmy Hightower."

"I will bring you to justice, Nate, for what you did, for what you have done."

"You'll have to kill your peers to even have a crack at me, Timmy. I doubt your sense of justice, of right and wrong is so bloodthirsty."

"If it takes these two boys to end this madness, Nate, I'm willing to do it." Timmy looked at his cards and threw a few chips in the middle of the table. "Boys, are you gonna place your bets?" Timmy glared at Carlos and Johnny before glaring back at Nate.

3.

Leopold smeared dirt and grass around his lips as he smacked them, the dull lightning still buzzing beneath his skin. He peered through the narrow slits of his eyes at the stoop of Timmy's parents' house before the dove landed in front of his face. Leopold clamped his eyelids shut.

"I know you're awake, Leopold. Don't worry, I won't tell Chief Donaldson." Leopold turned his head to face the doves.

"What…have you done?"

"I had to stop you from killing him. I need him as part of my operation."

"…what?"

"Did you think you were the only one working for me, Leopold? One must have multiple players, multiple options to go to in order to sustain and survive. How else did you think you got your case thrown out of court?"

"You…you had me save that guard's life…the one that…"

"I had to see if you were willing to let go of your anger despite the atrocities committed to your body and soul. Anger burns you out after awhile. While it makes you faster, stronger, braver, it also makes you really stupid. To work for me long term, you must have a great degree of control over your emotions. You've grown so much. As insurance though, he had orders to subdue you once the game began."

"The game…has begun?"

"Ten minutes ago, we lost sight of Timmy. When you started questioning whether Timmy should go through with playing the game or not, I had to ensure you wouldn't be a liability."

"You...bastard."

"Tsk, tsk. It's impossible for me to be a bastard when I have no father or mother. Motherfucker wouldn't work either since I didn't fuck mothers, just made a married woman a mother. Fortunately for you since I'm on this earthly plane, there's nothing I can really do to punish you. We're using quite a bit of bandwidth as is just to maintain control of this bird. I don't understand though why you're so angry. I'm the one who's risking his only son. The body he's in is just a shell."

"Timmy's still in that body, somewhere."

"Not really. If all goes according to plan, Timmy will get his body back. What's that? Really? Why couldn't you keep him away? Oh...oh crap. You've done all we have asked you to do Leopold and we appreciate everything you have done. Now, we ask you to do nothing, to allow the game to continue until it is finished. You've earned the right to sit back and relax. We'll be in touch, Leopold." The dove turned, flapped its wings, and darted toward the clouds.

* * *

"Why is my Uncle Leopold down on the ground in front of my house and in handcuffs?" The diving suit asked Peter and the giant television screen that showed a white dove and Leopold talking.

"He...he was going to hurt Chief Donaldson. We had

to stop him or else things would have ended really bad, Timmy. The Chief was the one who brought your uncle to justice, remember?"

"What justice? Uncle Leopold was acquitted."

"True, but when a man like your uncle gets a chance at revenge, he'll take it at the most opportune and inappropriate time."

"Peter, why are you lying to me?" Timmy closed the distance between it and Peter until the diving suit stood three inches away from him.

"Why…why would you think I'm lying to you?"

The diving suit balled its right fist and planted it into Peter's stomach. Peter collapsed, wheezing. "You've been lying to me this entire time, Peter, you and him. I think it's time I found out why." Timmy walked past the collapsed Peter toward the giant television screen.

"Stop!" Peter yelled, holding out his right hand, making a pulling motion at the diving suit's back. "Stop!" Timmy continued moving forward, uninterrupted. "I said stop!" Peter brought himself up to his feet. Timmy turned around, ran, then jumped, his flying foot detonating in Peter's stomach. Peter flew back, smacking against the adjacent wall. He slid down the wall to the floor, crumpled. Timmy walked over to Peter, bent down. He grabbed Peter's chin to get a good look at whether his eyes were open.

"What's going on here?" The dove landed on Peter's head. Timmy's hands lunged for the dove but got a part of Peter's scraggly, long gray hair. Timmy's head and body followed the fluttering of the dove's wings until the dove landed in front of the television screen. "Timmy, what have you done?"

"While you were doing whatever you were doing back on Earth, where you had me, the people that were around just disappeared. I started wandering around to find you and Peter. That's how I came in here. That's how I saw what you did to Uncle Leo and heard your conversation with him."

"Are you questioning my plans, Timmy? You know what happens when people question me."

"There's not a lot you can really do in that form. Peter's the only one who can get you out of it and he's out cold. I knew he'd alert you that I was here and I knew you'd make it back here as fast as possible."

"Do you really believe I can't escape this form or punish you from this form, Timmy?"

"Harm me and you harm your operation. You need to maintain the integrity of my soul in order to maintain access to my memories, my unique skill set."

"Not right now, I don't. I made sure your body was given an insurance policy that will guarantee victory. You're violating the terms of our deal, Timmy. I'm going to give you a chance to walk away. Do so, and I'll forget everything that happened."

Timmy walked over to the giant television monitor, stood in front of it with his arms extended out. Two columns emerged from the ground, the diving suit's hands fitting perfectly on top of each column. "Show me where my body is," Timmy said to the television monitor. The dove hovered in Timmy's face.

"What are you doing?"

"Testing your insurance policy."

The television screen showed Timmy and two other boys sitting around a table, holding black poker cards. In the middle of the table, there were three cards face up—7 ♦, Q ♠, and J ♣.

"Show me Timmy's hand." The screen revealed a 2 ♠ and 5 ♣. "That's a pretty bad hand, isn't it?"

"Yes. So?"

"This connection he has with me in order to maintain use of my body...I bet it's a two way street, isn't it? It can't be just a passive connection on my end and an active connection on his end. We're going to test my theory right now." Timmy gripped the columns, his body pushed all of his chips into the middle of the poker table, hands holding onto the chips. "It looks likes my theory is correct."

"Timmy, stop this. Stop this or else."

"Or else what? Once I make my hands take them off the chips, the bet is done."

"I will free myself of this form and send you, your grandmother, your parents, to Hell for your disobedience."

Timmy's hands stopped touching the chips and went back to his face down cards. "It's time to call your bluff." Carlos looked at his face down cards, then looked at the giant stack of chips in the middle of the table.

"You must be either really bad at this, Timmy, or you've got a killer hand. I'm not gonna get knocked out on the first hand." Carlos threw his hand at the empty black tin. "I fold."

"It looks like your plan is going to backfire, Timmy," the dove taunted.

"Why do you not sound so sure about that?"

"I'm sure of everything. You'll see."

Johnny's brow knitted and furrowed. He looked at his face down cards, then back at Timmy. "I don't buy it at all." Johnny pushed all of his chips in the middle of the table. "Let's see what we've got." The top card from the deck levitated and flipped face up after landing on the table: an Ace ♠.

"No need to wait to reveal the river card," Nathaniel said. "One of these boys is going to be ours in just a moment." Another card levitated, flipped face up: a 6 ♦.

"Call," Johnny said. Timmy revealed his hand. Johnny turned over his cards: a Q ♦ and a J ♠. Timmy twitched, the blood pouring out of his mouth turning his feet, then legs to stone. The boys and Nathaniel watched Timmy slowly become a statue.

"So much for the great boy detective," Nathaniel sighed. "Pity. I was looking forward to facing him."

Carlos clutched his chest, turned to the side and vomited breakfast with flecks of blood. The acne on Johnny's face cleared up, his upper lip sprouting a respectable teenaged brown mustache. Nathaniel pointed at the puddle next to Carlos. The puddle of vomit boiled, then burned away. "No need to have that sitting around."

"What have you done," the dove chirped. "You killed him."

"Now we're trying guilt? If my body was dead, why am I still able to see…"

The stone around Timmy's body cracked, flaking away. Timmy shrugged his shoulders, moved his arms and legs, shattering the rest of the stone around his body. A bronze bracelet appeared on Timmy's wrist for a moment before splitting, the halves diving into the pieces of stone that once surrounded Timmy's body. A fresh set of poker chips appeared in front of him, glowing white.

"Ah…that partially explains how two of the cards came back to me unclaimed." Nathaniel said. He opened his hand. The halves disappeared from sitting next to Timmy's chair into Nathaniel's hand. He peered over his glasses, inspecting the bronze bracelet. "Yes…this looks very familiar. Master, do you see what I see?" The loose cards shuffled into the deck, then the deck placed itself into the black tin.

"Yes…that was an invention of Hephaestus. This was on the boy detective?"

"It was."

"How?"

"I don't know. We could try and ask the boy to find out how this got on his wrist. You haven't seen this in what…over one hundred years?"

"Are we going to play or just listen to you and a deck of cards talk to each other," Carlos said. Nathaniel pointed at Carlos's throat.

"You won't need this for a bit." Carlos heard his own voice come out of Nathaniel's mouth. "Timmy has some outside help. We need to stop the game and leave, now."

"We can't. Once the game has been initiated, the game must continue until it is finished. No exceptions."

"I don't know if I can protect you. Something is really wrong here when a 12-year-old boy is wearing something that was invented by an ancient Greek god. You do see that, right?"

"Yes. But once the game has been initiated, the game must continued until it is finished. I'll be trapped, exposed until then. What can you do to protect us, Nathaniel?"

"Let's see if…we're being watched." Nathaniel took his glasses off. He pulled a red silk handkerchief out of his right inner pocket, cleaned the lenses carefully before putting the glasses back on. Nathaniel looked at Timmy, noticing a gold thread coming out of the back of Timmy's neck. "Someone is watching us through Timmy's eyes. I don't think I can find out who but I can at least get them to stop." Nathaniel thrust out his right arm, his hand open. "Blind those who dare lay their eyes upon this sacred circle." The monitor went black, then shattered. The diving suit collapsed. The dove landed on its chest.

"Timmy! Timmy!" The dove frantically cooed. "Where are they?"

"What…did you do? What have you done?"

"Our insurance was a degenerate, meth-addicted professional poker player. We managed to…borrow him and make him more useful to the world. He was going to help us win the game and gain control over the deck but because of your actions, my son's soul is in danger. Do you remember where they were playing, Timmy?"

"It…it looked like…they were playing in my dining room. I noticed over Carlos's shoulder the aged rooster clock above the sink in the kitchen. My mom loved that thing."

"We don't have much time. I'm flying back down there. You'll need to revive Peter to get him to fix the monitor."

The diving suit brought itself upright, started lumbering over to Peter's crumpled body. "Could… could his soul be claimed?"

"I don't want to find out." The dove frantically flew past the diving suit and Peter's body, through the double doors.

4.

Johnny's left eye struggled to stay open as he looked at his cards, then over at Carlos's side of the table where Johnny's chips stood tall.

"Only four hands in and we're so close in gaining another soul," Nathaniel said. "At this current pace, I might be playing the last boy standing in 30 minutes."

"Don't...count...on...it." Johnny slurred. "Call." Carlos revealed his hand, giving him a three of a kind Q (♥, ♠, ♣). Johnny's left eye opened again thanks to his full house—three 5s (♥, ♦, ♠) and two 7s (♥, ♦). "It looks like you spoke too soon, dickwad."

"You do realize I could shut you up like I did to Carlos, right?" Nathaniel cracked his knuckles one by one.

"Just shut up and play." Carlos said, waiting for his face down cards to land in front of him.

* * *

The dove landed on the roof of Chief Donaldson's police car.

"You need to let Leopold go. My son...my son is in danger. Timmy has thrown everything into jeopardy."

"How?"

"It's a little hard and long to explain right now, Chief, but let him go."

"I thought you could handle this sort of thing yourself."

"Normally, I could, but the magic within the deck prevents me from doing so. Leopold has a personal interest in Timmy's safety. He's the best one to handle this situation."

"He's going to kill me when I uncuff him."

"He won't." The dove flew off the hood of the car, landed in front of Leopold's face.

"Leopold…"

"I heard…everything. I promise…not to kill him. Where…is Timmy now? Do you know where he is?"

"They're playing in your house. Your nephew figured out how to access his body. Where I am unable to see in places where there is no belief in me, he was able to watch himself and the others play the first hand. We must hurry. The man they call 'Nate', the caretaker of the deck, knows Timmy had help. We don't have much time."

Leopold felt the bite of the handcuffs on his wrist ease, the ache in his shoulders rushing out. He rolled on his back and kipped up in one fluid motion. A knife landed in Chief Donaldson's left and right shoulder. Blood pooled beneath Chief Donaldson's uniform as he slumped against the grille of his squad car.

"Ow." Chief Donaldson tried to stop the bleeding with his hands but his arms wouldn't listen. He cocked his head toward the dove. "You made him promise…"

"I promised…not to kill you. I never promised… that I wouldn't hurt you. When this…is all over,

Chief, you, my knives, and I…are going to have a long conversation." Leopold pointed a knife at the dove. "And you…won't stop me." Leopold took the knives out of Chief Donaldson's shoulders, wiped the blades clean using Donaldson's pants before sheathing them. He turned away from the moaning, bleeding Chief and started running toward the front door.

5.

Nathaniel heard the front door fall. He turned to face Leopold and three flying knives. Nathaniel held his hand out, stopping the knives in midair. Nathaniel closed his hand and the knives dropped. "You must be Leopold. I remember watching your great great grandfather back in Oklahoma when the Fabulous Franzs toured all over the west and I see his skills have been passed down quite well." Nathaniel pulled out of his coat two obsidian knives. "I've always wanted to fight your family but as you can see…" he pointed his knives over to the boys sitting around the table, the deck levitating, dealing them their face down cards. "I've been busy."

"Well…" Leopold pulled two knives out of his vest. "This is your chance." Leopold and Nathaniel circled each other.

"Oooh…I wonder if you can fight without throwing…" Leopold lunged at Nathaniel's throat. Nathaniel stepped to the side, back to circling Leopold. "That was…" Nathaniel noticed a drop of blood on his shoe. He moved his clenched hand up to his right cheek, then looked at the back of his hand. "You…" Leopold jumped back, kicking Nathaniel in his kneecaps. Leopold kipped up, jumped on top of Nathaniel pinning his arms down with his knees, knives to Nathaniel's throat.

"What…were you saying?"

Nathaniel's obsidian knives glowed. Nathaniel disappeared from beneath Leopold, inside the circle with the other boys.

"I'm impressed. No one has been able to get the best of me in so long." Nathaniel picked up the deck, placed it in the black tin. "It looks like I'll have to end the game for now. Don't worry, all of you will still get to play. The game ends only when one of you is the last boy standing." Nathaniel placed the tin inside his coat, held the obsidian knives above his head. The knives glowed, the invisible barrier keeping the circle intact shattering. The boys, Leopold shielded their eyes with their forearms as the light within the circle grew brighter. Nathaniel and the deck disappeared. The bracelet that Timmy wore reappeared on the floor, intact.

"What happened here?" Chief Donaldson stumbled into Timmy's house, a dove perched on his shoulders.

"The deckholder escaped," Timmy said. "He figured out I had help." Timmy held up the bronze bracelet in front of the dove and Chief Donaldson. "What…is this?"

"It was supposed to be insurance," the dove cooed, "something to make sure you would win against the other boys and Nathaniel."

"Holy shit! That dove talks," Carlos said.

The dove flew onto Carlos's shoulders, pecked at his neck. Carlos collapsed. The dove then flew onto Johnny's shoulders, pecked at his neck. Johnny collapsed. "Enough out of those two," the dove cooed.

"Because of your meddling, he knows I had help. We're not going to be so lucky next time," said Timmy. "He'll change the pattern, add additional players. According to my research, the game must start from the beginning. If Nathaniel fails to do so, the deck starts losing potency."

"What…do you suggest," Leopold asked.

"I do this alone. No help from you." Timmy pointed at the dove. "Or you." He pointed at Chief Donaldson. "Or you." He pointed at Leopold "All of you have messed this up."

"But…"

"No buts, Leopold. You were following orders, I get that, but I can't have any of you interfering. If we're to reclaim those lost souls, we do things my way." Timmy handed the bronze bracelet to the dove, placed it in his beak. "Bring this back to where it belongs." The dove flew away, holding the bronze bracelet in his beak.

* * *

Nathaniel placed the black tin in the middle of the pentagram carved into the floor of the living room in an abandoned house. He stepped back. A column of red energy surrounded the tin. The tin levitated, crumpled, reshaping itself into a black goat.

"What have you done," the black goat bleated.

"I got us out of there while you were most vulnerable, master. We've been so successful over the last century or so by being patient and selective with our moments when to initiate the game. While children have made for better targets based on the potency of their souls, it's also made the risk of getting caught greater. People give a damn about dead children, even if they are awkward, middle school boys. We've done our best to minimize the attention based on the boys that the deck selected but now...we've attracted too much attention."

"Laying low is not an option, Nathaniel."

"Master, I know that. The game was interrupted. It must be finished before we can move on elsewhere but we must be selective when the game begins anew and where."

"What will you do?"

Nathaniel pulled a journal out of his coat, opened and thumbed through it, stopping when he reached a specific page. He brought the journal over to the pentagram where the goat could see.

"Do you have enough power to grant me to do this?"

"Nathaniel...what you want to do...I was only able to do once and it was out of desperation."

"Yes, to develop my predecessor rapidly. It wouldn't

require your energy alone to make this happen. I've honed my own magical skills quite well."

"You have, that is true Nathaniel. In all the eons I have witnessed humanity and what they are capable of, you are one of the rare few to be so naturally attuned to the arcane arts. However, the last time I did this, it almost killed me. Even if you combine your powers with mine, this could weaken us severely. You might not be strong enough to face the surviving boy that wins the game."

"I have a plan, master. We had only three players last time, one of which had someone's soul in a bronze bracelet. As long as we have the original physical players, we should be fine. We just need two more."

"Nathaniel, won't this attract more attention?"

"Not if we make it look like accidents."

"Alright. When can we get started?"

"Tomorrow morning during rush hour."

"In broad daylight? Why?"

"When was the last time you've heard of a 'secret' accident? To make it look like an accident, it has to happen at the most obvious time in a most obvious way. The police will focus on the most obvious cause, not the fact that it is tied to us or the game."

The black goat crumpled into itself, reshaping into the black tin. The column of red energy disappeared. Nathaniel removed the black tin from the center of the pentagram and placed it in his coat pocket.

6.

"Holy Hell! What happened here?" Chief Donaldson stepped out of his squad car, walking toward the cordoned off part of Highway 27. Asphalt dotted the Ford Explorer's cream colored paint job like a bloated, dying leopard, wheels spinning in the air. The seat belts in the front held the two bodies in place.

"Something tapped the car pretty hard and made it flip over a couple of times and bam, these two were dead right after the car stopped rollin' around the highway," Detective Bronston said. "Here's something really weird though, Chief: there's no blood at all comin' out of these bodies. Here you've got a major accident and you'd think with all the bruises and cuts, there would be blood somewhere on their bodies or comin' out of there bodies. Nothin'. Weirdest damn thing I've ever seen."

"Have you identified who they are yet, Detective?"

"Something else that's weird, Chief, is that the registration, their licenses, Hell, even the license plate is gone. We're gonna get them out and see if we can ID them using their prints. If we don't get anything, we may have to try IDing them with their dental records."

"We can't rule this as an accident then, can we, Detective?"

"No, sir, not with all this weirdness."

Chief Donaldson pulled out his iPhone, pressed a button, then put it to his ear. "I know he's in school and I can't pull him out of class. I need you to come to Highway 27, between Exit 55 and Exit 56. Bring a camera or a cellphone that can take pictures. Can you do that for me? See you in twenty minutes."

* * *

A polished cobalt blue El Camino pulled up beside Chief Donaldson's squad car. A man stepped out, walked toward the crime scene. Detective Bronston noticed the man's slicked back black hair, salt and pepper handlebar mustache, the tattoo creeping from the collar of his shirt as he came closer. Detective Bronston drew out the sidearm holstered on his hip and aimed.

"Freeze, don't you move! Don't you fucking move!" Detective Bronston felt Chief Donaldson's hand pressing gently on his shoulder.

"Lower your weapon, Detective. He's on our side."

"But Chief, that's the man…"

"…who was acquitted of all charges, if you recall. Everything you thought he did was alleged, never proven."

"But you, you said you saw him…"

"Fear makes you see things you want to see, not that you need to see. Now, lower your weapon. That's an order."

Detective Bronston holstered his side arm. The man made his way underneath the crime scene tape, stopped in front of Chief Donaldson and Detective Bronston.

"Chief…you wanted to see me?"

"Yes, Leopold. Did you bring what I asked?"

"The cellphone with…the camera? Yes."

"Good. I need you to take some pictures of the scene and send it back to Timmy's lab."

"He said…not to interfere."

"This isn't interference. The boy's in school. We found the car stripped of any way to easily identify the bodies. The detective found no signs of blood on the body like you normally would in an accident. I think…I think that Nathaniel is creating eligible players on his own. We might see more 'accidents' like this really soon. Like I said, this isn't interference. Timmy would want to know."

"You…are right. I'll take the pictures and send them back to his lab right away. Just…keep the detective away from me, ok?"

"Alright, Leopold. Go ahead and take those photos."

Leopold pulled the cellphone out of his pocket and walked closer to the turned over Ford Explorer. "How… are your shoulders doing," he asked over his shoulder.

"They're fine…just fine."

"That's good. Hopefully, you won't…get yourself into that situation again." Leopold aimed the cellphone camera, walking around and taking photos.

"Chief, what situation is he talking about?" Detective Bronston asked.

"Nothing you need to be concerned about, Detective. Let's get this mess cleaned up. Give the coroner's office a call and let them know they can send someone to retrieve the bodies. This needs to be on the top of his list. We need a cause of death, and quickly."

"Chief, what's going on?"

"I've got a bad feeling this is tied to another open case. I've got a bad feeling that Timmy Hightower's gonna confirm that my bad feeling is right on the money. I've got a bad feeling this won't be the last accident we see that looks just like this."

* * *

"Sir…"

"Have you got the monitor fixed yet, Peter?"

"Yes, I have. That's what I wanted to talk to you about. Two people died a few minutes ago and these people clearly believed in you but…"

"You can't seem to find them here."

"How did you…"

"Peter, did you really think that yesterday morning, the game would play out entirely?"

"I did. We followed your plan to the letter and everything was supposed to play out as you planned it."

"But it did. I expected Timmy to figure things out, to question you, to even attack you. I expected him to be smart enough to figure out the two-way connection between him and his physical form. I expected him to throw a monkey wrench in my plan. I expected Leopold to go after Nathaniel the way he did and get incredibly close to killing him. I expected Nathaniel to run after coming so close to death. I wanted him to know that Timmy had help from a possible extraordinary source."

"You put your own son at risk."

"I had to. The panic I felt once Timmy went all in on that hand and lost was quite real. If the game continued and my son lost his soul to Nathaniel, that would have been the end of us all. You should know by now that I only tell you what I need you to do as part of all of my plans. As long as you do what you are told on your end, everything else falls into place, as it always does."

"What's your intention then?"

"When an opponent is scared or spooked, he tends to take bigger risks, make bigger mistakes. Time is now working against Nathaniel. The longer he waits to resume the game, the more likely the deck starts feeding on his soul. Instead of allowing Fate to do its job, Nathaniel is now acting as an agent of Fate. There could be dire consequences in circumventing the deck's natural selection process, something I'm counting on when the game resumes."

"Your son, though, has no idea how to play poker. And Nathaniel was able to see how Timmy's body was tethered to something greater than himself. How are we going to provide support this time to ensure your plan is successful?"

"Who said we're going to provide support, Peter?"

"What?"

"You heard my son. He asked for no help this time, that he would do this on his own. If he wants our help, he will need to ask for it, and at some point, I'm sure he will. Where is Timmy right now?"

"I managed to sedate him. He's in the lab with Soriano."

"Excellent. When the time is right, the next phase of my plan will begin. We can't have Timmy interfering this time. Until then, keep watching the monitor and check in with Donaldson, Peter. We must keep track of who dies over the next couple of days and who doesn't make it up here after they die."

"What will you do until then?"

"See if I can get some of our assets in Afghanistan to provide us some more resources. We'll need all that we can get for this next phase coming."

Chapter 6

1.

Carlos rolled off the anvil just as the hammer came down, blood coming out of his ears after the clang.

"I'm sorry. I didn't see you there. Let me help you up."

Carlos looked past the extended hand, noticed the sweat dripping from the man's beard and brow, how he leaned slightly on his cane, how the man went from being fifty feet tall to six feet tall. Carlos felt the heat and calluses in the man's palm as he brought Carlos back to his feet.

"Where am I?"

"My boy, you are in my workshop."

"Which is where?"

"Where? Where? My boy, you know the answer to this already."

"Ok, enough with this weird shit, Nathaniel."

"Who's Nathaniel?"

"Who's Nathaniel? You know who he is, you prick. He's you. You're Nathaniel and you're fucking with my head."

"I'm not this 'Nathaniel' my dear boy, not at all. That fall must have scrambled your brains more than I thought."

"Are my shears ready yet, Hephaestus?" A woman cloaked and hooded in gray appeared in front of Hephaestus.

"Not quite, Atropos. My assistant here…had a bit of a nasty fall. It might be a couple of more hours."

"Blacksmith, a couple of hours is unacceptable."

"Atropos, you know how everything ends. Didn't you or one of your sisters see this happening?"

"Now you are being glib and rude, blacksmith. You forget I have the power to end you."

"Only when it is my time, threadcutter. Only when it is my time."

"What the fuck is going on here? Who are you two? Where am I?"

Atropos pulled a strand of hair out of Carlos's head. A pair of scissors materialized in Atropos' left hand. She opened the scissors and placed the strand of hair between the blades. "You will have all the answers you seek in time, Carlos. In time." The scissors snapped the strand in half.

Carlos fell through the floor of Hephaestus' workshop, emerging from the comforter he bunkered beneath. He looked around, breathing heavily. The Metallica and Slayer posters were where they belonged in Carlos's bedroom. He pinched his forearm, winced at the pincer of his forefinger and thumb. Carlos threw the comforter off the bed, stomped over to his trenchcoat draped over the chair pushed into his desk. He pulled out whatever was in each pocket. Carlos searched through the debris of crumpled notebook paper, gum and candy wrappers, the tangled headphone cord for his iPod. "It's not here. It's not here. If it wasn't Nathaniel then…" Carlos stuffed the debris back into random pockets of his trenchcoat before draping it back over the desk chair. He walked over to the comforter, put it back on his bed, straightening the crumpled mass before sliding back beneath it. Carlos stared at the ceiling fan, hoping the cool air, the spinning blades would lull him back to sleep.

* * *

"Sir, I think you need to see something." Peter pressed a button to rewind the screen before pressing another button. Carlos was in bed one moment, disappeared for a few minutes before reappearing in bed. "Did you see? Did you?"

"Yes, Peter, I saw. How did he disappear like that from our view?"

"I don't know, sir. I was hoping it was part of the plan."

"It isn't."

"It isn't because you won't tell me for sure, or it isn't because it actually isn't?"

"It isn't because it actually isn't. I don't know how Carlos disappeared from our view like that."

"What now?"

"Get Chief Donaldson to keep close tabs on the boy. More and more, he's becoming trouble. We need to minimize as many variables as possible, understood?" Peter nodded. "Good." Peter walked out of the room, leaving Carlos disappearing and reappearing behind on the screen as a loop.

2.

"Timmy, it has been awhile since I've seen you in class." The old Korean man stood in front of Timmy, staring at the five alarm Taco Dog halfway in Timmy's mouth, glaring at the dripping chili and cheese.

"Um…" Timmy gulped the rest down, wincing at the heat of the chili and molten cheese smothering his throat. He sipped his large half cherry/half vanilla soda. "…Master Shim. Hi, yes, I'm sorry Sabumnim, but I've been dealing with the death of my parents and this case."

"That's no excuse, Timmy, no excuse at all. Training helps focus the mind, body, and spirit in situations such as these. In your grief, I see you are stuffing your face with this American swill. Get up. Get up, now, and let's see how much of your fighting spirit you still possess."

"Sabumnim, I don't have time for this. My uncle will be here any second. We're heading over to the police station to take a look at…" Timmy raised his forearm in time to shield his head from Master Shim's axe kick. Timmy got off the bench and into fighting stance. Timmy and Master Shim circled each other.

"Not bad, Timmy, not bad at all. I see you still remember…" Master Shin closed the distance between them with a spinning roundhouse kick, Timmy raising his forearm in time to block Master Shim's instep from crushing the right side of his face. "Why won't you hit me, Timmy? Has your grief weakened your killer…" The knife grazed Master Shin's chest before shivering in an adjacent tree. Master Shim looked down, watched the tear widen on his track suit, watched the hint of blood pooling beneath it. Timmy looked to his left and saw Leopold walking closer toward them.

"Uncle Leopold, what are you…"

Leopold grabbed the Tae Kwon Do master by the collar and flipped him onto an empty table. Leopold crouched over Master Shim, holding one of his throwing knives to Master Shim's throat.

"Lay a hand…lay a hand on Timmy again…and I will…" Leopold's knife trembled.

"Uncle Leopold, they're gonna call the cops on you. Let him go. We need to get out of here." Timmy walked over, squeezed Leopold's left shoulder gently. "He's not worth going to jail for."

"What's going on here?" Timmy and Leopold looked up at the two cops aiming their guns at Leopold. "Sir, you'll need to put the knife down."

"This man…was attacking my nephew, officer. He needs to understand…to never, ever do that again."

"Is this true?"

"He was…just testing me but…he went too far. See." Timmy showed his left and right forearm where Master Shim's kicks landed. "I haven't been to class in awhile. My uncle saw him attack me and did what he thought would be best."

The cop standing closest to Timmy brought his

sunglasses lower on the bridge of his nose to get a better look at the scene. "You're Timmy Hightower, right?"

"Yes, sir."

"Bob, it's ok, it's Timmy Hightower and his uncle. The Chief's expecting them back at the station."

"Really? I mean the guy's got a knife to the other guy's throat, shouldn't we do something about that?"

"Swear…you won't touch the boy…again."

"I swear. I swear. I swear."

Leopold placed the knife in his vest before jumping off the table and walking over to the two cops and Timmy. He turned, placed his arms and wrists behind his back. "Officers…I'm sorry. Do…what you must."

"Sir, are you willing to press charges?" Master Shim shook his head, still sobbing and rubbing his neck. "Then, we're good. You both can ride in the back of my squad car." Timmy and Leopold head towards the squad car. The cop with the sunglasses turns back to face Master Shim. "Sir, I hope you have a good day."

* * *

Leopold, Timmy, and the two officers accompanying them walked into Chief Donaldson's office.

"What took you so long?" Chief Donaldson puffed his pipe.

"Does Master Shim ring a bell, Chief?" Timmy asked.

"That's your Tae Kwon Do teacher. Why?"

"Master Shim decided to spar with me outside of Taco Dog. Uncle Leo put a stop to it in the only way he knew how."

"Is Shim alive?" Leopold nodded. "How bad did you hurt him?"

"Just…a small cut. Enough…for him to never do that again."

"Did he want to press charges?"

"No, Chief," said the officer wearing the aviator sunglasses.

"Even if he did, we'd still drop 'em. Guy's a prick. You two can go now. And shut the door behind you." Chief Donaldson pulled out four manilla folders from his desk, opened them. "Eight other deaths on the highway today, each a couple. Tires punctured. Out of control car tapped just right to flip over a few times, somehow killing them. No blood was found at the scene or in their bodies. Matches how Marie Swanson's parents died."

"He only needed two more players. Did all of the couples have children?"

"One couple had no children at all, the others had children, but not your age." Chief Donaldson pointed at one of the manilla folders. "The Johnsons have a 23-year-old daughter. The Hintons' son is 37. The Dunklestone's twins died in labor."

"This doesn't make any sense. He's straying from the pattern big time. This isn't like Nathaniel to be so careless."

"Ten murders matching from where it happened, how it happened, how the bodies were found, that's going to bring a lot of attention, press, the state police, Hell, the Feds might get involved with this because of the unique nature of the crimes. Once word gets out that we've got a serial killer in town, everyone is gonna panic. This isn't careless at all, Timmy. This is intended to overwhelm our resources, overwhelm everyone so when he does restart the game, no one will notice a few children disappearing. We might need to ask for some assistance to keep this quiet."

"You mean…"

"Yeah. Only your dad's got the kind of power to make all of this be not so visible for a short time. Eventually, we'll have to tell the truth or at least our version of the truth. You still want to do this alone, Timmy?"

"It looks like…it looks like I can't."

* * *

"Did you hear that?"

"I did, Peter, I did. The prodigal son has come around. How many of them didn't make it up here?"

"Just the Swansons. Everyone else made it up here and they're in the battery where they belong."

"Excellent. Our assets did quite well on this operation and we used a minimal amount of our resources to execute it. In fact, we gained some resources. All in all, not bad. Not bad at all."

"What now?"

"Is everything repaired, Peter, from that brawl you and Timmy had?"

"Just finally got everything fixed."

"Good. It's time my son and I have a little talk. Since he needs my help, I'm going to ensure he asks nicely."

3.

Nathaniel took out a sterling silver pocket watch and one of his obsidian knives from his right inner coat pocket. He opened the watch, placed it on the table. The knife made a small incision on his wrist. The first drop of blood covered the *12*, the second the *6*. The third drop of blood landed in the middle of the watch. Nathaniel closed the watch, passed the flat of the blade over his wrist, sealing the wound. He picked up the watch and dropped it in a bucket of blood in the middle of the table. Nathaniel stepped back, pulled out the other obsidian knife, and pointed both at the bucket of blood.

"Master, are you ready?"

"I am."

Black, sickly red light spilled from the black tin, Nathaniel's obsidian knives. The bucket of blood trembled, the blood boiled, simmering. Nathaniel sucked some air, held the knives steady. The bucket stopped trembling. Nathaniel sheathed the knives, walked over and retrieved the pocket watch from the now empty bucket. Nathaniel opened the watch, the numbers on the face coated with crimson and chrome.

"It's time to test this, Master." Nathaniel stuck one of his knives where the bucket once sat then walked away. "Whenever you're ready." Nathaniel opened his right hand, his left thumb pressing down on the pocket watch's winding stem. Nathaniel walked four paces to his right before pressing down on the winding stem again. The knife flew from the table into the wall. Nathaniel walked over, removed the knife and placed it back into the coat.

"What just happened, Nathaniel?"

"I have made my watch strong enough to place objects in between time. Once I remove the field from the object, then time moves at its normal speed."

"How long can the field last?"

"Depends on the size of the object. That knife could have spent days in the field before it finally broke. With small objects, the watch has enough power to do that. With larger objects though, we'll have an hour or two before the field breaks."

"The knife didn't move though."

"Right. The knife didn't move because it was between time. However, had we also been between time, the knife would have flown at me without hesitation. The watch has always had two functions. The only way I've been able to take down a posse was to slow them down or speed myself up to be just fast enough to get the drop on them. The watch has enough power to place a field around a room. Outside, time will move at normal speed. Inside the field, one hour equals eight, more than enough time for the game to finish uninterrupted and for us to escape."

"You are sure this will work?"

"We don't have a choice. I sense you weakening, my power weakening, especially after completing the ritual. We'll resume the game unnoticed very soon thanks to a copycat killer."

"A copycat killer?"

"Yes, I know you've slept to conserve your energy so our link isn't as strong as it normally is but someone killed four other couples the same way I killed the Swansons. I wasn't able to determine who. Someone or something bigger is helping Timmy Hightower. This countermeasure should prevent such interference."

"You realize what will happen if you fail, Nathaniel."

"Yes. You will be crippled and I'll be dead. I already feel twenty years older and slower. I've kept death at bay for over a century and I plan to keep it that way. Now please, conserve your strength. We will need all that we have left if we want to survive."

* * *

A dove landed outside of Timmy's bedroom window, pecking at the glass. Timmy turned toward the sound.

"Go away," Timmy moaned.

The dove continued pecking at the glass. Timmy covered his head with his pillow, the beak against glass still getting through. The dove pecked, scraped his beak against the glass slightly, then pecked. Timmy turned back toward the window, throwing the pillow away. He rolled out of bed, walked to the window and opened it. The dove flew inside, perching on top of Timmy's desk.

"You couldn't have just telepathically said you were here? I mean, I don't know how the boy understands Morse code like that."

"He's a boy detective. They're required to know arcane languages in order to solve mysteries, like the one Timmy solved involving a jewel thief that received his jobs via telegraph," the dove cooed. "Besides, in this form, I am limited in how I can communicate. I asked Peter to make sure I could at least talk. However, Morse code was the best way to wake the body up. I understand you are in need of my help."

Timmy rubbed his eyes. "I am. There were ten people murdered in the exact same way. Did any of their souls make it over to you?"

"I had Peter check. They never made it up."

"Then Nathaniel had something to do with all of these deaths. I think he's using these murders as some sort of distraction. He knows that causing so many deaths in the same way is going to draw attention—the local and national media, the state police, possibly the FBI. This is so big that it'll force the Chief and all of his resources to focus their attention on the case. While all of this is going on, no one will notice five children disappearing until it's too late."

"And you want me to hide what's happened?"

"For a day or two. We can't let Nathaniel and the deck escape."

"I thought you didn't need any help, my boy."

"I was wrong and I'm sorry I said that. Please, help me."

The dove pecked Timmy's desk a few times before looking back up at Timmy. "I'll do everything that I can to hide this." The dove flew off the desk and landed on the open windowsill, then turned to look at Timmy. "Thank you for trusting me to help. I know our relationship hasn't always been that great, just know that everything I've done, everything I do, is in your best interest. Remember that." The dove turned away from Timmy and flew out of the bedroom.

4.

"Hello, Carlos." Carlos looked up at Hephaestus looming over him. "I apologize. Let me make myself a little more human." Hephaestus shrinks himself down to being two feet taller than Carlos. "Coming back for another visit again, I see."

"What am...what am I doing here?"

"Searching for answers, boy. Your subconscious is at least. Don't you want to know about what drove your parents..."

"No, stop. Don't even say it. They were disgusting assholes."

"The boy isn't ready yet." A woman cloaked and hooded in gray appeared in front of Hephaestus and Carlos. "He's not ready to know the truth."

"Atropos, you and your nonsense about destiny needs to stop."

"It was destiny that brought this boy to life. It is destiny that he is here in this time and place. There are no coincidences."

"What is she talking about?" Carlos rubbed his eyes.

A clank echoed throughout Hephaestus' workshop.

"We may not have time to answer that question right now." Hephaestus stroked his beard. "Any moment, you will wake up."

Another clank echoed throughout Hephaestus' workshop.

"Mr. Francisco. Mr. Francisco. Are you still with us, Mr. Francisco?"

Hephaestus' workshop shook, stalagmites split against his anvil. Atropos calmly stepped to her left, debris landing where she once stood.

"You cannot ignore your past, Carlos, if you want to see your future. Remember this. Remember this if you want to…"

Carlos threw his head back, loudly sucked in air. The rest of his third period American History class stared.

"Mr. Francisco, so nice of you to finally join us. Does my Teapot Dome Scandal unit bore you?" Ms. Ewing, the rest of the class snickered. The croquet mallet balancing on her shoulders was wrapped in a sticker version of the American flag.

"I'm sorry, Ms. Ewing. I didn't sleep well last night."

"That's no excuse, Mr. Francisco. You know what the penalty is for sleeping in class." The bell tone piped through the speaker above the chalkboard. Desks, shoes scraped against the linoleum, the noise cutting out Ms. Ewing.

* * *

"Timmy...I need to talk to you."

Timmy Hightower closed his locker, turned to face Carlos. "Are you here to taunt me, Carlos? Because if you are, I don't have time for it."

"Actually...I need your help." Carlos leaned into Timmy's right ear. "And your father's help. Meet me in the corner of the lunchroom. If anyone asks, you're interviewing me about a case. Timmy isn't normally seen talking to the likes of me." Carlos walked backwards, yelling, "I can't believe you would actually think that I would be the one to put laxatives in Mr. Zachen's green tea, Timmy Hightower. That is amateur bullshit. You might want to talk to one of the sixth graders trying to make a name for himself. Next time you come to me with a wild accusation...just you wait and see."

The warning bell tone piped through the speakers

in the hallway. Carlos turned away from Timmy and sprinted before the hallway clogged with rush minute traffic.

*   *   *

Timmy waded through the sea of snorting, chomping, and giggling of Parker Lewis Middle School's second lunch shift for Carlos and the skin of his black trenchcoat. Timmy ignored the "hey mans" and "wassups" until he reached the far corner of the lunchroom, where Timmy watched Carlos devour today's taco salad special.

"I can't believe you eat that swill." Timmy said, putting his tray down. "What's that meat made of? Orphans?"

Carlos dropped his fork. "That's…not like Timmy to make such a comment, or you for that matter."

"I thought you might appreciate the attempt at humor."

"Well…that was actually pretty funny. I think those raging hormones are finally starting to make you a little more human."

"What did you want to talk to me about, Carlos?"

"Does the name Hephaestus ring a bell?"

Timmy leaned back for a moment, looking up and to the left, then looked at Carlos. "Nathaniel mentioned him when he discovered the bronze bracelet someone put on me during the game, also mentioned that he made the tin that housed the cards. What about him?"

"I've been having these weird dreams where I appear

in his workshop and he wants to tell me something but there's always this woman who stops him and says I'm not ready to know the truth."

"Who's the woman?"

"Ah…Ah trop…Atropos."

Timmy leaned back again. "Atropos…Atropos is one of the Moirai. She was the one responsible for choosing how someone would die, cutting the thread weaved by her sisters when it was that person's time to die."

"I've talked with them twice now, last night, and during American History. I have a feeling I'm going to see them again the next time I sleep."

"Is there anything they said that might clue you in why you keep seeing them?"

"Before Ms. Ewing woke me up, Atropos said 'You cannot ignore your past if you want to see your future'."

"You don't have much of a past. You're 12."

"I know. I know. I don't know where to start."

"Let's lay out what we know. Nathaniel and the cards named Hephaestus as the creator of the deck and of the bracelet that allowed my body to hold an additional soul. When did you start having the dreams?"

"The night after everything happened."

"My theory is that the presence of the tin, of the bracelet, triggered something dormant in you. Your life is somehow entwined with these two gods and you have to figure out how."

"Did you get a chance to talk to him?"

"Uncle Leo did, actually. When you are dreaming of Hephaestus and Atropos, you disappear from his view."

"Huh?"

"My father can only see those who believe in him, or those who at least acknowledge he exists. These dreams you have…make you invisible while you're in that state. He's freaked out about it, about you. You're a variable he can't control and he hates what he can't control."

"Is that why he sent Leopold to my house to scare me?"

Timmy blinked hard, his neck and face shook. "What?"

"Your Uncle Leo showed up to my house a few nights ago. The card I received protected me from him. I thought you sent him but Timmy has always been able to handle his own business, one of the things I grudgingly respect about him. You had no idea did you?"

"No. And I'm sorry."

"No need to say sorry. At least I know who really sent him. I need to stay asleep. Suggestions?"

Timmy stroked his chin for a moment, then drummed his fingers on the table. "Check the medicine cabinet at your foster home."

"And get kicked out of another foster home? No thanks."

"There might be another way. Come over to my house tonight."

"What?"

"You heard me. Come over to my house tonight."

"What about your rep, your popularity? You have to maintain a certain appearance of credibility, don't you?"

"I'm working a case. I think everyone at this school gets that by now, don't they?" Carlos nodded. "So, come over to my house tonight. Bring something comfortable to wear."

"We're having a sleepover on a Tuesday night?"

"Not exactly."

* * *

"Leopold! Leopold! Where are you?" Timmy dropped his backpack next to the front door. "We need to talk, Leopold." Timmy stomped through the living room, the dining room. A thunk faintly reached into the kitchen, between the storm of Timmy's sneakers. Timmy looked through the window above the sink facing the backyard at Leopold rolling toward the oak tree, coming out of it in a kneeling position, then a knife shaking in the trunk. Timmy opened the sliding glass door to the backyard, yelled "Leopold!" as he walked outside. Leopold turned, right arm half cocked, a throwing knife between his fingers.

"Timmy...what are you doing here? You should be at school."

"I snuck out during lunch. What else has my father ordered you to do?"

"What…are you talking about?"

"Carlos told me you paid him a visit a few nights ago."

"He's…"

"Don't even say what I think you're about to say, Leopold, because he's got no motivation to lie to me. I'm going to ask you some questions and you're going to nod or shake your head to answer, do you understand?"

"Timmy…"

"Not another word. Understood?" Leopold nodded. "Good. The bronze bracelet, you put it on me the night before the game, correct?" Leopold nodded. "You were somehow responsible for acquiring the soul that was in that bracelet, correct?" Leopold nodded. "You were going to pay another visit to Carlos soon, weren't you?" Leopold nodded. Timmy looked up at the sky. "What is wrong with you? Seriously, what is wrong with you?"

"My orders…were to protect the boy's body, to protect you. I was doing…as I was told. You of all people… should understand that."

"I chose my destiny, Leopold, and I have no regrets about the choices I made, just as you chose your destiny. I didn't do what I was told. I was presented information and decided the best course of action.

"I made a deal. I must…continue honoring that deal, Timmy, for my own good, and to some extent, yours. He gave me a second chance and I am grateful for that."

"What about what you did to Master Shim outside of

Taco Dog?"

"That was…all me. He…had it coming."

Timmy walked back to the open sliding glass door, turned to face the backyard and Leopold. "I know right now that you can't disobey his orders. I don't know the price you'd pay for doing so but I know it would be high, possibly even your life. You have yet to face the consequences of your actions, Leopold, and one day you will have to face them. You can't avoid what you have done forever. You'll need to see to it before he does, and once you are useless to him, he will, deal or no deal." Timmy slammed the sliding glass door shut. Leopold walked over to the oak tree, removed the knives stuck in the trunk, and sheathed them in his leather vest.

5.

"It is done." Hephaestus' voice rumbles out of John Mason's mouth.

"Hand it over so I may inspect your work." Mason hands the black box to the man wearing a gray cloak, holding his cane in his left hand as he looks over the box carefully. He whispers and various runes appear all over the black skin before they fade away. "Well done, blacksmith. You and your host have done well."

"Thank you. About what I asked…"

"Ah, yes, the terms of our deal. I cannot cut the string of Fate binding you and Atropos. One day, you will destroy each other, no matter how hard you wish to deny it, but I can lengthen the twine between you and her, allowing you to not be found for awhile. There is a price for this. You will have to give up some of your strength and this will bind you to your host until he dies. You will not be strong enough to choose your next host. They will have to choose you, willingly or not. This host will figure out a way to protect you though so you can survive until your next host finds you. Do we have a deal, blacksmith?"

Mason extends his right arm and opens his hand. "We have a deal." The gray cloaked man takes a knife out and cuts Mason's palm. "Ow, shit, what did you do that for?"

"Keep your hand open," the gray cloaked man hisses. Mason keeps his hand open as the gray cloaked man dips the tip of his cane into the blood before grinding the tip into the ground. "Arrows of Apollo, wound the vision of Fate so she may not see Hephaestus." Mason staggers, falling to his right knee and then his left as the top of the cane glows brighter. The light ceases. The wound on Mason's palm knits itself shut. "It is done, blacksmith. Enjoy the rest of his life."

* * *

"Carlos. Carlos. Are you ok?" Carlos's eyes fluttered open, the back of his head throbbing. Timmy stood over him, arm extended, hand open. Carlos reached up, Timmy pulling him to his feet. "I saw you walking up to the front door and then you just collapsed on the sidewalk."

"I had another vision. Hephaestus was speaking to…I think a wizard. Hephaestus was in a man named John… John Mason and they talked to each other, the wizard about some sort of deal."

"Why does that name sound so familiar?" Timmy stroked his chin. "Was anything else said?"

* * *

"What does the inventor of the Mason jar have to do with all this?" Timmy asked aloud as Carlos sat next to him in front of Timmy's computer in Timmy's basement office/crime lab before turning his office chair to Carlos. "Or better yet, why did Hephaestus, or your subconscious show you this?"

"So I can understand my past in order to see my future. But what am I supposed to understand?"

"What triggered you fainting outside of my house?"

"I don't know. I was walking up to your place and all of a sudden, you're helping me up."

"Then we need to get you back in the trance somehow. While we figure that out…Leopold! Come in here for a moment." Timmy and Carlos listened to the squeak of floorboards, then the creak of stairs as Leopold walked into Timmy's crime lab.

"Yes…Timmy."

"We need to talk with John Mason. Can you ask my dad to make that happen?"

"I can try. I thought you and him…weren't on

136

speaking terms again."

"To a certain point, we are. I asked him to redirect all the attention those 'accidents' created and so far, he's done so quite well. I think if we can talk to Mason directly, we can find out how the tin works, how to end the game quickly without death."

"I'll…see what I can do." Leopold turned, walked up the stairs. Halfway up, he turned to look Carlos in the eyes. "What happened the other night…I'm sorry. I was only…following orders." Leopold turned his back to Carlos and walked out of the crime lab.

* * *

"Peter, what did we do with John Mason?"

"What are you talking about?"

"John Mason. I thought you as the gatekeeper kept tabs on everyone that came up here."

Peter pulled out a PDA, pressed a few keys with his thumbs. "Um…he was a host of Hephaestus, right?"

"Based on what we have heard, yes…oh. That would have been too easy, wouldn't it?"

"It would have."

"Then I've changed my mind about the boy. Make sure Carlos is protected until this is all finished. When Leopold comes calling, give him the bad news and the order, understood?" Peter nodded. "The little troublemaker might be the very key to our salvation."

*   *   *

Something blunt and metal struck Carlos in the back of his head. He fell out of the office chair, onto the island of carpet in Timmy's crime lab. Timmy turned, saw Leopold with his left arm extended. Timmy stood up.

"What did you do that for?"

"It was the easiest way to get him…back to dreaming as deep as he needed to. If I threw it right…and I'm pretty sure I did…he'll be out for hours."

*   *   *

Carlos raised the sword above his head, the force of the blow driving him to his right knee. Carlos pushed the blade on the woman's arm away. She staggered, allowing Carlos to get back on his feet and catch his breath.

"Atropos, I will cut you out of there," the woman hissed, her voice rumbling like a volcano. Carlos looked at the sword in his hand, looked at the woman's brown hair tied back in a ponytail, her brown eyes.

"Mom?"

"Atropos, you finally lost your mind after these centuries. That won't stop me from killing you." The woman pointed the blade on her arm at Carlos. "Are we going to continue?" Carlos pointed his sword at the woman before widening his stance and circling her.

"How…how am I doing this?"

"Doing what, Atropos?"

"This. I've never used a sword before."

"Wait." The blade on the woman's wrist retracted into the bronze bracelet. She walked over to Carlos and placed her right index finger and thumb on Carlos's temples. "I will help you get where you need to go." The woman caught Carlos as he fainted. She lifted him and laid him down on the brown leather couch, stroking his hair.

* * *

Atropos drove the xiphos into the neck of the kneeling blacksmith, melting into his body. The skin around the entry wound sealed itself, leaving no scar. Atropos noticed Carlos watching in the corner of the blacksmith's workshop. She walked over to him as the blacksmith convulsed on the floor.

"Hello, Carlos. What have you learned so far?"

"Was my mother…a host to Hephaestus, like Timmy's a host?"

"Timmy is more of a shell than a host, but you already knew that, didn't you?"

"Are you real or is this all coming from my imagination?"

"Yes."

"To which question?"

"Yes."

"Why can't you give me a straight answer, or why can't I give myself a straight answer?"

"I know how the thread ends, Carlos. It would be foolish for me to share that with you. You would worry about where and when it ends rather than living your life."

"You call dealing with your parents murdering each other a way to live?"

"They would have died sooner or later, Carlos. Step into the hearth."

"Um…"

"It will take you to what you need to see next. Hephaestus didn't harm you, right?"

"No, he didn't."

"Then step into the hearth."

Carlos walked over the moaning blacksmith and into the hearth, fire and ash swallowing his body.

* * *

Sarah knelt, her left forearm attempting to stop blood and smoke escaping from the long slit in her belly.

"What have you done, Atropos?"

"Once my blade touches you, I control the wound. All I did was make it longer." Atropos' hollow, hive of hornet voice came out of Tom's mouth. "Now, you kneel, bleeding out your life and hers, Hephaestus. I must make sure there's no escape for you." Tom took the sword out of the floor and pressed a button on the hilt. The sword and hilt split, forming shears that Tom pointed at Sarah's bracelet. "Your time is up, Hephaestus." Tom walked over to Sarah, cut the bracelet off of her wrist. Smoke poured out of Sarah's eyes, mouth, and stomach wound.

"Atropos, you said you could help her."

I can't until Hephaestus is completely gone.

The last trail of smoke seeped out of Sarah's stomach. "Tom…he's gone. He's finally…" She collapsed on the floor, her blood forming a lake beneath her body. Tom turned Sarah over.

"Sarah? Sarah?"

"Tom, you…did…it. I'm finally…free."

"Hang on, Sarah. I'm gonna get you help. Atropos can fix this, she said so."

"You've…already…fixed this. Tell my dad…I'm sorry."

"Sarah…there is still time for us."

"No there's…not. Who wants…to live…forever?" Sarah shuts her eyes.

"Sarah? Sarah? No. No! Atropos, fix this. Fix this now."

Had you obeyed me from the beginning, Tom, done as you were trained to do by your father and his father and so on for thousands of years, I would undo this. There are penalties for disobedience, Tom, and they are severe.

"Dad never told me about penalties."

He never had to. The rules you were to follow have always been in you, as they were in your father and so on. You are the first to resist, to question.

Tom grabs his punctured shoulder. "What are you doing?"

Giving you back the ability to feel pain. Feeling every blow, every stab and passing out from all the pain and blood loss is just the beginning.

"Damn...you." Tom fainted. A moment later, Tom got back on his feet, sword in hand.

"I don't have much time." Tom walked into Sarah's bedroom, opened Sarah's closet. He pointed the sword at the back of the closet. The closet rumbled for a moment and then stopped. "That takes care of Hephaestus' pocket universe." Tom walked back into the living room, pointed the sword at Mario's body.

It unraveled as smoke. Tom propped Sarah's body in a kneeling position. He stood behind her, sword raised. "I'm sorry that this is the best I can do."

* * *

The crash of the waves, the sun slapped Carlos awake. Atropos, wearing a gray hood stood over Carlos.

"Now, do you understand?" Carlos nodded. "What do you understand?"

"My mother was a host for you and for Hephaestus."

"Very perceptive, Carlos. Very perceptive."

"May I ask a question, Atropos?"

"You may. I may not give you a straight answer though."

"Is why I'm seeing you and Hephaestus because of both of you using my mother's body at some point in her life?"

"Partially."

"Am I imagining all this or are you both a part of me?"

"Yes." Fissures appeared in the sun, causing pieces of it to break away and fall. The ocean turned into lime green Jello. "Our time is up for now, Carlos." The sand softened beneath Carlos, savoring his body as he sank.

* * *

Carlos jerked upright in the office chair, howling silently and thrashing.

"Carlos…Carlos…you're back. Calm down." Leopold gripped Carlos's shoulders. Carlos tried breaking Leopold's hold, striking Leopold's forearms with his.

"Carlos, it's ok. Leopold won't hurt you." Timmy stood in front of Carlos.

"Really? The bastard threw one of his knives at the back of my head."

"It was…the only way I knew…to knock you out the way…you needed to be knocked out. If I wanted to kill you…you would be dead."

Carlos stopped thrashing in his chair, in Leopold's grip. Leopold released Carlos's shoulders and stepped back.

"How long was I out?"

Timmy looked at the clock on the computer, turned back to Carlos "20 minutes."

"Can you put me out again? For longer?" Carlos asked Leopold.

"What did you see," asked Timmy. "What did you see?"

"My mother. I saw my mother—she wore the same bronze bracelet that you had on during our game—dying in the arms of a man named Tom. Her name wasn't my mom's name, it was Sarah. My mom was...like Timmy's body, a host. My mom was the host of Hephaestus and I think she also hosted Atropos. I need to go back and find out though for sure."

"What about the tin? Anything about the tin or the cards?"

"Not this time. They don't want me to know more about the tin right now."

"How do you know that?"

"Because...I don't want to know more about the tin."

"Our souls are at stake, Carlos, or have you forgotten?"

"I haven't, Timmy. I haven't. But I think finding out more about where I came from will help us with what we're dealing with now."

"What are you saying?"

"I'm the child of two gods."

"That's...not possible."

"It is. There were gods before your father, before you. They were the last remaining of their kind, one running from his fate, one executing her last duty. My mother hosted both and what was left of them was transferred into me. It's because of them I saw through your shell and knew who you really were the moment you talked to me. I think the lack of having them made my mom crazy, trying to recreate her death constantly to try and get whatever was left of them, if anything, to surface."

"That's quite the leap in logic."

"So's believing in someone who came back from the dead three days after they died."

"As opposed to believing that there was a god for every single thing that existed?"

"Boys," Leopold interrupted. "We don't…have time to argue. Carlos, what do you want to do?"

"I need you to knock me out again. For hours. Can you do it?"

"Can I? Yes. Should I? No."

"I don't care, Leopold. Do it. I'll deal with a headache."

"Timmy…"

"Do as he wants, Leopold."

Leopold pulled out a throwing knife from his leather vest, putting it between his right index and middle finger, making sure the butt of the grip jutted out. "Carlos, are you ready?"

"Yes. Do it."

Timmy watched Leopold's right hook slow to a stop, the butt of the grip hovering an inch away from Carlos's temple.

"Timmy, what's going on?" Carlos watched Timmy fade away from his crime lab before everything slowly disintegrated before Carlos's eyes.

6.

"What's the boy's status, Peter?"

"Aware and sedated just like you asked."

"Excellent. Get him plugged in."

"What about Leopold?"

"He's no good to us right now. I'm not sure if this will even work, Peter."

"But I thought you invented time?"

"I did. I set the parameters, the limitations. The first couple piloted it after they fell into temptation. It's the one thing that is always reliable in providing us with what we need to keep things running. This magic, this creature…I guess I wasn't thorough enough in ensuring I was the only one left. I thought I did everything I could to make magic and superstition unacceptable and foolish to reduce its potency. I was wrong."

"Everything will work out. As you say, have faith."

"Faith won't help us this time, Peter. We must rely on luck."

*   *   *

"Wake up, boys."

Timmy and Leopold lifted their heads, rubbing their eyes. Nathaniel sat on the other side of the table, sleeves rolled up, shuffling the black deck.

"What happened to you?" Timmy pointed to Nathaniel's graying black hair, the crow's feet nesting deep around his eyes.

"Time is finally starting to catch up with me. Don't worry, all of you will help fix that."

"All of us?" asked Carlos.

In the chair next to Nathaniel appeared a girl with a blonde hair pageboy cut, bangs just above her eyebrows, wearing a black dress.

"Hello, Marie." Nathaniel said over the shuffling of the cards.

"What…what am I doing here?"

"You were chosen, Marie, chosen because of the loss you've endured. This is your chance to bring your parents back. All you have to do is win."

"Marie, he's lying. Playing this game will cost you your soul," Timmy said.

"Of course you would say that, Mr. Hightower, especially with that crush you've had on Marie for quite awhile."

"What crush?"

"If you lie this bad, I doubt you'll last long in the game." Johnny Decarn materialized in the empty chair between Marie and Nathaniel. "Oh good, our last player has arrived."

"Oh shit, it's you."

"Where's the fifth player," Timmy asked. "There's always five players. You normally come after the game ends to challenge the winner, unless…"

Nathaniel placed the shuffled deck in the middle of the table. The deck levitated, dealing each player two cards. The deck landed softly. Poker chips appeared in front of everyone around the table.

"Ladies and gentlemen, it's time to place your bets."

"Leopold is going to find you again, like he found you last time."

"Leopold didn't find me last time. I know he had help, but don't worry. No one will interfere with us this time." Nathaniel pulled out a sterling silver pocket watch, placed it next to the deck, and pressed down on the winding stem. "We are now between time. When the game is finished, I will exit this field and re-enter normal time. We have more than enough time to play."

"I refuse to play."

"There's a penalty for not playing once you have been chosen, Timmy. Only one can leave this game. Do you really want to take that chance?"

Timmy picked up three chips from his stack, threw it

in the middle of the table. "Let's play."

Chapter 7

1.

Carlos peeked at his face down cards (7 ♥ and 7 ♠) before the cough erupted from his throat, the blood spatter stopping below the cards in the middle of the table. He looked up at the statue of Johnny Decarn, the wobbling stack of chips in front of Marie. Timmy and Nathaniel breathed punctured. Nathaniel pressed the button on top of his sterling silver watch opening it, stared into the face before sealing it shut. "How much time is left?"

"Enough." Nathaniel raised a closed hand to his mouth, catching his cough.

"For who?"

"Would you both shut the fuck up and play?" Marie yelled, sliding a stack of chips into the pot. The boys looked at their hands before throwing them down in disgust. Marie revealed an Ace ♥ and a 2 ♥, making a two-pair with the Ace ♦ and 2 ♦. Marie's blonde hair shimmered, the blemish on her right cheek disappearing.

"You're looking a little low there, Nate," Carlos said, pointing at the shallow stack of chips in front of Nathaniel. The deck shuffled itself, cut, reformed, levitated. "How long do you think you'll last by continuing to fold, Timmy?"

"I haven't had the right hand yet." Timmy peeked at his face down cards—King ♥ and King ♠.

"Awwww, Timmy's feelings for me won't let him hurt me. That's so adorable," Marie hissed.

"You've never been this bitchy before," Carlos sneered.

"Would you all shut up?" Nathaniel said, throwing three chips into the pot.

"You won't be hearing us much longer." Marie shoved one of her stacks into the pot. "You'll pay for what you did to my parents." Marie pointed at Timmy. "Don't worry, I'll save you for last. You at least deserve to look at me one last time, before I take your soul."

She...is worthy. The words buzzed in Nathaniel's ear.

2.

"Any luck locating them?"

Peter leaned forward on the console. "There's this kind of blank spot here. I think this is where the game is going on."

"His power must be waning if he's that sloppy. Give Chief Donaldson the coordinates and tell him to bring

Leopold. Have you done as I asked about Timmy?"

"I have. What you've proposed is risky. This could destroy both of them."

"Let me know when Donaldson and Leopold are at the location."

* * *

Leopold and Chief Donaldson stepped out of the cobalt blue El Camino, staring at the translucent purple column surrounding the abandoned tire factory.

"We're here," Chief Donaldson shouted to the air.

"How…do…we get through that?"

"Take two of your knives out and hold them high." Leopold turned to the dove's coo, the skittering of its claws on the hood of the El Camino. Leopold removed two knives from his vest, pointed them to the sky. Lightning struck the two blades, streaming from the clouds. "Now, aim them at the field." Leopold forced his arms down, aiming them at the abandoned tire factory. The lightning pried a hole through the field.

"How…"

"No time for questions, Leopold," the dove cooed. "You have about two minutes before the field repairs itself.

Leopold sheathed his knives, ran to the abandoned tire factory, and jumped through the opening. Leopold kipped up and watched the field knit the tear shut.

* * *

The field has been breached.

"How," Nathaniel whispered to his face down cards.

Timmy's uncle…he found a way to get through.

"He can't breach the field surrounding the game. We're safe."

You are dying. It might be time…for new blood.

"Stop it." Nathaniel threw five chips into the pot. "Call." Nathaniel watched Carlos and Marie reveal their hands, smiling.

* * *

Leopold walked through the abandoned tire factory, knives out. Leopold ducked as a knife came out of the shadows, quivering in the support beam behind him.

"I don't know how you made it in." Nathaniel stepped out of the shadows, holding an obsidian knife. He stretched out his hand. The knife behind Leopold shook, then flew into Nathaniel's open palm. Leopold backflipped, three knives released from the arc. Nathaniel pointed his knives downward. Leopold's knives fell in front of Nathaniel's feet. "That was slower than I expected." Leopold lunged. Nathaniel stepped aside, cracking Leopold in the back of the head with the handle of one of his knives. "That was just…" Nathaniel looked at the throwing knife stuck in his right shoulder, before grabbing it and throwing it aside.

Leopold kipped up, knives in hand. "The monster…

bleeds."

*   *   *

Nathaniel grabbed his right shoulder, took off his glasses.

Choose. Now.

Nathaniel shoved all of his chips into the pot. "Call."

Carlos revealed a pair of 10s (♠, ♣), pairing with the three 7s (♠, ♣, ♦). Nathaniel's suit and skin began cracking, blood trickling down the fissures.

"Well…played," Nathaniel gurgled. "I hope…you are the last man standing. You…owe me a rematch." Nathaniel's suit and skin exploded, Timmy, Carlos, and Marie shielding their eyes. Timmy peeked over his forearm, noticing the slump in the statue's shoulders, the frozen waddle of its neck.

"I can't believe it. I killed him," Carlos said.

Marie leaned over and punched Carlos in his right arm. "You asshole. He was mine."

"It's not my fault your hand wasn't…" Carlos watched boils inflate all over Marie's arms, hands, face.

"Thhht wsnt…Nthnl," Timmy slurred.

Nathaniel reeled back, sidestepping Leopold's thrust.

They know.

"Good." Nathaniel deflected the knife flying at him.

You are using too much of what you have left. End this.

Nathaniel planted his knives into the floor, held out his arms. Leopold flew backwards and slammed into the wall on the other side. Nathaniel walked over, stared at slumped, moaning Leopold. "Time to get Timmy into the game." Nathaniel grabbed Leopold by his hair and started dragging him.

3.

"I can't see much right now," Peter leaned forward, squinting at the screen.

"But you can see something," the air hissed.

"I can." The ceiling crawled, leather scratching against cement came through the speakers.

* * *

The deck dealt Timmy, Marie, and Carlos their face down cards. Timmy's right hand shook furiously as he reached for his cards.

"What do you mean that wasn't Nathaniel," Carlos yelled.

"Lk hat thstht."

Carlos watched a body slam into the side of the forcefield behind Timmy, the energy rippling against the impact.

"Hello players." Timmy, Marie, and Carlos turned towards the voice. "I'm impressed you were able to eliminate my proxy, Carlos. I'll show you what I can do to you when my attention is undivided soon enough."

Nathaniel walked close to Timmy. "Your chip count is becoming dangerously low, Mr. Hightower."

"Lt m'wry bt tht."

"You weren't worried enough, and that concerned me, until…" Nathaniel picked up Leopold and slammed him face first into the forcefield, pinning him. "I caught your uncle. I could kill him in front of you, but what fun would that be."

"Wh glt."

"Let me make it easier to understand you." Nathaniel pointed at Timmy. Timmy's tongue shrunk to its normal size.

"Why gloat? You caught him. Just kill him so we can get back to playing."

Nathaniel dropped Leopold. "I'm going to offer you a great opportunity, Timmy, one that may very well save your life and Leopold's. You'll have to survive Marie, Carlos, and then me, of course. As I said your chip count is dangerously low. I can bring it back, give you a fighting chance."

"That's not fair," Marie yelled.

"What are you offering?"

"The use of Leopold's soul. Win, and you both get something you want. Lose, I get both of your souls."

"I don't need it. I just need the right hand."

"You can't win by being a pacifist. The cards maim. The cards kill. The sooner you accept that you have no control over what the cards can do, the better you can play this game."

"Do...it," Leopold moaned.

"You heard the man. He's willing. Are you?"

"Leopold, I can't risk you."

"Please...do it."

Timmy peeked at his face down cards. "I accept your offer."

"Leopold, place your hand on the forcefield," said Nathaniel. Leopold placed his right palm on the forcefield. A stack of ink black chips appeared in front of Timmy. Each chip had an ever changing blood spatter pattern roving the surface.

* * *

"I see Timmy. I see the other two children. I can even see Nathaniel. Leopold looks bad."

"Excellent. Timmy needs to stay alive long enough for the next part of the plan. Do we have the energy to do it?"

"I need one more hour to gather it."

"Do what you must."

* * *

Timmy turned over his face down cards, revealing pair of Jacks.

"But..." Marie's eyes, nostrils flared. Blood trickled

from her right nostril, then her left. The trickle became a pour. "No…you won't let me die, will you Tim?"

Timmy pushed himself out of his chair. The chair legs moaned against the floor. He stepped backward, stopped near the forcefield keeping the two of them playing. A tear fought its way out. "I can't stop it."

The blood seeped from Marie's forehead, her eyes. "Tim, I'm sorry. I don't deserve to die. Not like this." Marie stopped bleeding once her face was dyed in it. The calcification crawled up Marie's feet, then calves. "Tim, please…say something." Timmy turned his back to Marie, covered his ears. "Tim, say…".

"Wow, that was cold." Nathaniel adjusted his glasses. Timmy turned back to face the poker table. Carlos glared at Timmy over his dwindling stack of chips before getting up from his seat.

"It was either her or me, and you know it couldn't have been me."

"You motherfucker." Carlos rushed Timmy. Timmy unleashed a roundhouse kick, his foot landing flush against Carlos's right temple. Carlos's eyes rolled back for a moment before collapsing to the ground.

Nathaniel walked over to Carlos, knelt next to Carlos's head and slapped his face. "Come on you little bastard, wake up." Nathaniel took his watch out of his jacket's inner pocket, looked at it, gave Carlos's face another slap. "Come on, wake up."

"Guess we can't play now, can we?"

* * *

"Welcome back."

Carlos looked at the stars. He felt sand spreading across his back and neck. "Where am I?"

"You have always been here," the stars gathered a beard, a mustache, mouth, eyes. "You were here before you knew you were here and you will be here after. You hold the hammer and tongs, the thread between the scissor."

"Why did you make the tin, the cards?"

"I was asked, and I was afraid."

"Of what?" The beard, mustache, mouth, eyes disassemble. Carlos looked at the scissors. "What am I?"

"A boy and not a boy."

The stars shake, whispered, "Wake up, goddamnit, wake up."

"You will see."

* * *

Carlos felt Nathaniel's hand clenching his shirt. He opened his eyes, grabbed Nathaniel's hand. "Let go of me, you creepy fuck." Nathaniel pulled Carlos to his feet, brushed his collar off.

"Welcome back. Let's continue."

Carlos looked at the tin, the language glowing and pulsing all over it. Carlos extended his hand. The tin rattled and jerked before levitating from the table, floating towards Carlos. Nathaniel grabbed the tin in mid air. The language seared Nathaniel's palms, escaped his grip. The tin stopped, hovers in front of Carlos. "You," Carlos points at Nathaniel. Timmy heard the rumble within Carlos's "You."

Nathaniel threw two of his obsidian knives at Carlos. They stopped next to the tin, stabbed the floor. "Who... what are you?"

"I am the one who made the shell and the skin for the soul that you aligned yourself with. You cannot harm me as long as you are aligned with this soul." Carlos pointed at the floating tin.

"I thought you died," the tin hissed.

"What is here now is the very last of me." The language on the tin glowed brighter. "I curse the day I allowed my fear to give you shelter."

"Shelter? Shelter? You created my prison. You drove me to kill to live."

"While I may have created your prison, you chose to kill. I must atone for all the deaths I have allowed to happen." Carlos pressed a couple of the glyphs on the tin. "Nathaniel, I hereby release you from this creature's custody." The tin and Nathaniel fell. Timmy watched wrinkles carve into Nathaniel's face, the brown in Nathaniel's hair bleed out.

"What..." Nathaniel stared at the liver spots spreading on his hands. "What..." Nathaniel wheezed, fell.

"Thank you. Whoever you are, thank you. ," Timmy

said.

"You know who I am. What is left of me is in this boy because of you."

"What are you talking about?"

"The son is the father. The father is the son. That is the way you wrote it. That's the only way this is done." Carlos pressed all the glyphs on the tin, summoning the cards on the table back into the tin. He shuffled the deck, drew five cards, placed them face down on the floor.

"Is the game still on?" Timmy noticed the fissures growing within the forcefield surrounding the table. "The forcefield is disappearing. It's over, Carlos. We can both go home."

Carlos stared at Timmy. "Marie can't go home. I can't go home. Let's see whether you will." Purple light crept from the cards, worked its way up Timmy's legs, into his mouth, down his throat. Timmy twitched, shook. Timmy heard Leopold yell his name as the room disappeared around him.

* * *

"Where is he?" Peter pressed buttons on the console. The monitor showed Leopold helping Carlos up from the ground, the two child statues, bones. "Where is my son?"

"He's gone."

"Well, find him! Gather all of our resources. We need to find my son."

"We're up against magic that existed before us. It's up to your son and Timmy to work their way out of where ever they are." The room roared, cracking all the monitors.

*   *   *

Timmy held onto the handlebar above his door as the pearl colored Range Rover rolled down the freeway. The front seats of the car were empty. The car stopped rolling. Through the windshield, Timmy saw an old diving suit holding the Range Rover still. Timmy looked at his hand, unbuckled his seat belt, and crawled out of the open window. He brushed himself off and straightened himself in front of the diving suit. "What are you doing in there?"

"Your friend Carlos gained control of the deck. Whatever was deep inside of him used it to send us here. He thought he was hurting my father."

"Where is here?"

"I wish I knew."

A house sprouted beneath their feet. Grass grew square by square from the asphalt, until it surrounded the house. Timmy flailed his arms. The diving suit arms squealed, lunging for the space Timmy once stood in. The diving suit inched its way to the edge of the room. Timmy rolled to his side, gets on his hands and knees, stands up slowly. He brushed the grass and dirt from his shirt, moved his left arm, his right arm, his left leg, his right leg. The diving suit jumped off the roof, lands kneeling in front of Timmy. Timmy looked at the house.

"That's my house, alright. I never fell off a roof though."

"I did. When my arm healed itself after the fall, that's what made me start questioning everything, who I was, why I never felt my father was really my father."

Timmy looked at the horizon, how the clouds hung stale. "It's safe to say that this place is constructed from a composite of our combined memories. The Range Rover was the last place I saw my parents alive. Does Purgatory work like this?"

The diving suit shrugged. "What's Purgatory?"

"Of course you wouldn't know."

The house collapsed. The remains formed into a model city six square feet wide, three feet high. Timmy and the diving suit walked over, watched the bustle of the model city, the inspection of fruit and farm animals. Timmy waved. The citizens don't notice him or the diving suit eclipsing the sun.

"This looks too modern," the diving suit said. "The clothing, the language, it's wrong."

"The language?"

"It's Italian. The people in this city are speaking Italian."

"That doesn't look modern."

"I didn't wear what they wore when I was alive." The diving suit looked up. "What are you trying to make me see?" The model city collapsed, the remains forming a door on the ground. The door opened, revealing a steel staircase. Timmy started toward the door. The diving suit placed both hands on Timmy's shoulders.

"What are you doing?"

"I don't like the looks of where that goes, Timmy. I don't want to go, and I don't want you to go."

"You came back from the dead. What are you afraid of? Hell?"

"I'm afraid of this place."

Timmy faceed the diving suit. "You performed miracles, so many miracles, brought the dead back to life, and yet you are afraid of a door in this weird, alternate dimension. What are you hiding?"

The diving suit's faceplate and hands glowed. "I'm hiding nothing." The diving suit aimed his arms at Timmy. "And you shall face my wrath for questioning me." Timmy shielded his face and chest with his forearms before the beam of light slammed into him, knocking him back. After the smoke cleared, the diving suit sees the mirrored glass that has taken over Timmy's forearms. Timmy leaped forward, lands a flying left cross on the diving suit's face plate. Timmy followed up by crouching beneath the diving suit, springing an uppercut that snapped the diving suit back, staggering. Timmy ran, planted a flying front kick in the diving suit's gut, sending it to the ground. Timmy sat on the diving suit, fist cocked, the mirrored glass skin of Timmy's forearms hardening into iron.

"Your father...he must have programmed you with safeguards in case something like this happened. He doesn't want you to remember something, but what?" A piece of the horizon landed just above the diving suit's helmet. "Are you doing this?"

"I'm not."

* * *

"I found them! I don't have a clear visual though," Peter said.

"Do you know how we can get them back here?"

"We'll have to overload your son and use that energy to bring them back from where they disappeared to."

"Do it."

Peter broke the glass around a red button, slams it down.

* * *

"Timmy?" Carlos and Leopold watched Timmy fade into the room. Timmy noticed the two small statues, the well dressed bones. "Timmy, where...did you go?"

"I don't..." Leopold noticed blood tricking from Timmy's nose. Timmy collapsed to the ground, shaking.

* * *

Timmy opened his eyes to find a dove pecking his chest.

"Good to see you're finally awake," the dove cooed.

"I'm…I'm still here. Why?"

"You were supposed to retrieve the deck."

"You…never told me that was why I was here."

"I shouldn't have to. That deck could have set us free from depending on souls for our continued existence."

"What was left of Hephaestus and Atropos saved my life. Even after his death, Hephaestus still did what was best for you."

The dove's eyes glowed red. "You have forgotten your place. When you are ready to give up on humanity, I'll let you come home."

"Don't punish Timmy for what I've done."

"Both of you have sinned. Both of you must atone."

* * *

Leopold Franz watched Timmy Hightower's eyes flutter beneath his eyelids before snapping open.

"You're…awake. Thank God…I thought I lost you… again."

Timmy looked around his hospital room. He noticed Chief Donaldson standing next to Leopold. "Timmy's not here."

✠

Cases

The Freshly Squeezed Slugger

"This...how..." Officer Jones looks around the kitchen, the wallpaper and tile stained with chunks of Little League uniform, blood. His latex glove covered right hand holds back the vomit from coming up.

"Awwww, what's wrong rookie?" Chief Donaldson walks into the crime scene, pipe lit. "Can't handle a little..." The pipe falls into an isolated puddle of blood. "Holy...Hell. What the Hell happened here?"

"I dunno, sir. I was hoping you could..." Officer Jones gags, holds back another wave. "I was hoping you could figure that out."

"I don't think...I'm the right person to do that, Officer Jones. I keep the lights on, keep the public off your backs when one of you mess up. I think it's time to call for some outside assistance on this one."

"Couldn't…our detectives handle this?"

"One's on vacation, the other's out on maternity leave. We're short staffed and I believe this was your career path, wasn't it Officer Jones?"

"Yeah, it is, but not…not like this."

"Then make the call, Jones."

* * *

"What do we have here?" Timmy Hightower stands in the door of the police station. Officer Jones stands up from behind his desk.

"Hi, you must be Timothy Hightower."

"Please, call me Timmy." Timmy walks over to Officer Jones' desk and shakes his hand. "I understand you've got a case for me."

"Yes." Officer Jones hands a manilla folder to Timmy. "Do you know Sergio Connor?"

"He was the star third baseman of the Taco Dog Devils, the national Little League champions. Saw him around in school here and there but never talked. We didn't run in the same circles. Why?"

"We found him yesterday…juiced."

Timmy opens the folder, looks at the photos. "Juiced?"

"Juiced."

"And you're asking me…to figure this out? Don't you

have detectives better equipped to deal with this kind of case?"

"The Chief recommended we bring you in on this."

"Have you tried figuring it out, Officer Jones?"

"I'm…I'm not ready for this kind of case."

"And you think I am?"

"Not me. The Chief."

"I guess I have no choice if Sergio has a shot at seeing any kind of justice."

* * *

"Have you…thought of asking him for help, of talking…to the boy?" Leopold Franz, knife thrower extraordinaire, asks Timmy.

"I can't. I'm still locked out up there. I'm lucky that I figured out how to access Timmy's skills again. I don't think my father realizes that yet."

"Your father…"

"Don't say it, Leopold. He might be listening."

"What's…his plan?"

"To see if I stop believing in the good of humanity, that they weren't really worth dying for after all. He'll keep throwing these kinds of cases at me until I stop believing or until I find a way back home." Timmy opens the manilla folder. "This boy was…juiced…for some reason. I have to find out why, Leopold. I haven't regained full access to Timmy's memories though so I need your help.

Who would have the biggest motivation to kill Sergio?"

"Hmmmm…" Leopold twiddles his handlebar mustache. "I have…an idea."

*   *   *

Timmy looks through the binoculars at the people sitting around the closed casket burial of Sergio Connor.

"The person…who looks the least sad that Sergio is dead…is our prime suspect." Leopold says over Timmy's shoulder.

Timmy watches Cara Connor, Sergio's mom. Her oversized black sunglasses muffled any signs of grief she had, her dress equally black, not muffling her figure. Theo Connor, Sergio's older brother, clutches at his mother, soaking her forearm with his tears. Timmy looks around the crowd, all of them grieving at various volumes until he notices a boy Sergio's age trying to grieve but slightly giggling beneath his hand.

"Leo, is that boy…laughing?" Timmy hands Leopold his binoculars.

"Yes…yes he is."

"Who is he?"

"That's…Travis…Travis Evans. He was the star third baseman for the Taco Dog Devils…before Sergio came along."

"He might be our guy then. I'll have to have a talk with him."

*   *   *

"Hello, Travis."

Travis turns around from his open locker to face Timmy Hightower.

"I heard what happened, Timmy, and I understand why you would suspect I did it. Yeah, I hated Sergio, a lot. I spent years, years working my way up the food chain. Sergio just walked in and…just had everything I spent so long trying to have a tenth of. He was too good."

"Do you have an alibi, Travis?"

"Yeah. I was home playing Dungeon Crawlers with my younger brother when that happened."

"Got a problem if I check that?"

"Nope, no problem. I wanted to beat Sergio fair and square."

"Why were you laughing then at the funeral?"

"Come on, he got juiced. Don't you see the irony in that?"

*   *   *

"Travis' alibi checked out, Uncle Leo. What now?" Timmy chomps down on a Five Alarm Taco Dog, the chili cheese sauce escaping the hard corn tortilla shell.

"You've got…the mother…and the younger brother to talk to."

"I think I need to look at the crime scene up close. I

have a feeling Officer Jones missed something."

"Are you...sure?"

"I'm not twelve, Leopold, remember?"

* * *

Timmy looks around the kitchen, the ghost of the blood and chunks in the blender. He looks at the police report. "Really...no fingerprints? How are these people allowed to be police officers?" Timmy walks upstairs to look around the bedrooms. Before walking into Sergio's room, he notices a bloodied aluminum baseball bat sitting outside of the master bedroom. "How did Officer Jones miss this?"

* * *

"Hello, Ms. Connor." Timmy sits on the hood of Ms. Connor's white Volkswagen Golf.

"Timmy...what brings you here?"

"Chief Donaldson asked me to work on finding out who killed your son and I was wondering if you could answer a question for me." Timmy holds up the bloodied baseball bat encased in a plastic bag. "Would you like to tell me how this was sitting outside of your room?"

"And what is that exactly?" A police siren blares closer and closer.

"Don't bother trying to run, Ms. Connor." The police car pulls up and Officer Jones steps out, gun drawn, aiming at Timmy. "Why did you do it, Officer Jones?"

"That kid was stopping us from being happy, Timmy. His obsession with baseball, the constant training, the money she had to keep spending. He had to be stopped. We were going to ship Theo off to his father due to him being so traumatized over Sergio's death and then live happily ever after."

"So you would blend him to death instead of being supportive of Sergio's dreams? What is wrong with you two?"

"You'll never find out."

A knife flies out of the bushes and plants itself in Officer Jones's hand. Leopold tackles Officer Jones, holds a throwing knife to his throat.

"No, Uncle Leo, don't do it."

"I've…killed before."

"But you haven't for 12 years. Don't do this. We got them."

Leopold sheathes the throwing knife as the police sirens come closer. "How do you…how can you keep turning the other cheek despite this madness?"

"I have to believe, Leo, I have to keep believing in them or all hope is lost."

The Early Bird Gets The Shaft

"Will this work," Nick Bishop asks, forcing himself to stand still against the wall.

"As long as you don't move, Mr. Bishop, I should be able to get it," the shadow across the room replies.

"I…I…I've changed my mind." Nick turns, takes a step. An arrow lands beneath his raised left foot, the shaft shaking.

"That was a warning, Mr. Bishop. You signed the contract. As far as we're concerned, this is happening. If you read what you signed, then you're already aware of the consequences should you walk away."

Nick steps back, extending his arms against the wall. "Alright, let's get this over with."

* * *

"Timmy, thanks for coming." Chief Donaldson shakes Timmy Hightower's hand.

"Of course, Chief. What seems to be the problem here?" Timmy turns and sees a man slumped against the adjacent wall, his hospital gown blood soaked, the darkest stains around the collar and stomach. "How did it happen?"

"Jim, can you bring the bag please?" A crime scene technician walks over, hands Chief Donaldson a large evidence bag with two bloodied arrows. Donaldson holds the bag in front of Timmy. "Our suspect might be a little too into those *Lord of the Rings* movies or something."

"Or something." Timmy takes a picture of the arrows and the body with his cell phone. "What's his name?"

"Nicolas Eugene Bishop. He was 39, a systems analyst. No wife or kids."

"Any enemies?"

"We just found the body thanks to a call to 9-1-1 from a nearby payphone."

"Let me guess…my father wants me to take this case."

"You guessed right, kid."

* * *

"I thought…I was the only one who preferred…never to use guns." Leopold Franz sits on the couch in Timmy's crime lab, sharpening his throwing knives. "At least… there was a body this time."

"Yeah. This time." Timmy turns to his computer, closes his eyes. He presses a few keys, opens his eyes again. "Looks like I figured out how to access the data miner Timmy uses to do deep research. The connection of Timmy's body to his soul is repairing slowly." The monitor brings up a picture of a man wearing horn rimmed glasses, slicked back brown hair. Timmy clicks the mouse, presses a few more buttons. "Leopold, the autopsy on Mr. Bishop. hasn't come back yet, right?"

"Your phone…hasn't vibrated or rang."

"I'll let them discover that he had stage three pancreatic cancer."

"Suicide…or a friend granting him his last wish?"

"I don't think a lot of people want to die by arrow, Leo." Timmy pulls up pictures of Nick Bishop's body. "Most of the blood came from his abdomen and the wound looks to be approximately where the pancreas would be. The neck wound though, that came second." Timmy presses a couple of keys, accessing Nick's bank statement. "The last transaction was three days ago. $700 to a TNSM Industries." Timmy opens another window, enters TNSM Industries in the Search field, hits the Enter key, then stands up and stretches. "Hungry? It's four for one night at Taco Dog."

"No, thank you. I'll stay here…and make a sandwich."

Timmy grabs his blue track jacket and New York Mets

cap hanging from the wall. "I'll be out for an hour or so. If that thing gets a hit, call me please."

An arrow flies through the open basement window and stabs Timmy's hard drive. Leopold leaps from the couch, throws three knives through the window before a second arrow impales the monitor. Leopold doesn't wait for the archer's scream to run up the stairs, outside the house. Leopold watches a white windowless van peel away. He notices a trail of blood leading to the curb where the van was parked. Leopold runs back into the house, picks up the phone in the kitchen.

"Hello?"

"You need...to come back...to the house."

"I'm in the middle of eating."

"Bring it back...with you. You need...to come home. I'm your guardian. You are supposed to do...as I say, remember?"

*   *   *

Timmy stares at the arrows stuck in his hard drive and monitor. "What happened?"

"Someone...shot two arrows. I threw...a few knives... got whoever it was. He escaped...before I could catch him."

"Was there any blood?" Leopold nods. "Why didn't you call the police?"

"I had to make sure...you were safe."

Timmy pulls out his cell phone, takes pictures of the ruined hard drive and monitor. He then presses one on the keypad. "Chief, bring a CSI team to my house. I'm sending you the pictures now."

* * *

"It looks like you were getting close to something," Chief Donaldson says as his CSI team pulls out the arrows, places them in an evidence bag. "Someone did their homework on you."

"How fast can you find out who it was with the blood?"

"If the shooter committed a previous crime, not long, but if someone is smart enough to figure out how you work, they're smart enough not to get caught. You can come to the station and use our stuff until you get your computer fixed."

"Thanks, Chief."

"The crime lab analyzed the arrows. The one we took out of Bishop's stomach, the head is made of depleted uranium. The one we took from his neck, the arrowhead is just steel."

"Before my computer was assassinated, I found out Mr. Bishop had stage three pancreatic cancer. Based on where you pulled out the arrow and what the head was made of…Chief, I don't think this was a murder. I think this was alternative medicine gone wrong."

"What are you talking about?"

"According to his bank records, Mr. Bishop paid $700 to a company called TNSM Industries three days before we found the body. That was the last significant transaction he made. Pancreatic cancer is one of the hardest cancers to treat and the survival rate is incredibly low. Mr. Bishop was trying to see if targeting the pancreas directly with radiation would actually work. Something went wrong and whoever did this had to put him out of his misery." Timmy opens the web browser on his cell phone, enters "arrows + medical treatment." The guitar solo from "Wango Tango" plays as the website pulls up. "Hey, Chief, ever heard of the Ted Nugent School of Medicine?"

* * *

"Thank you for seeing us." Leopold, dressed in a tan cardigan sweater, a white buttoned up shirt and khakis, shakes the hand of Dr. Elias Harington, the dean of the Ted Nugent School of Medicine. "Shake the man's hand, Frank." Timmy, wearing a New Jersey Devils baseball cap backwards, black bags under his eyes, leans up from his wheelchair to shake Dr. Harington's hand.

"It's my pleasure. How were you referred to us?"

"I watched a YouTube video of one of your patients, Erin Grant, delivering a testimonial. She had breast cancer in her right breast and thanks to your methods, her cancer went into remission. She posted the link to the school's website and well…I'm desperate."

"Excuse me for a moment, please." Dr. Harington

picks up the receiver of the black phone sitting on his desk, presses a couple of buttons. "John? Yes, it's Elias. Ms. Grant supposedly posted a testimonial about the school on the Internet. Would you please investigate and determine whether she violated her contract? Thanks, John." Dr. Harington hangs up, turns his attention back toward Leopold. "Desperate? How so, Mr. Merkel?"

"My boy here," Leopold places a reassuring hand on Timmy's right shoulder, "Has a brain tumor that's resisted all forms of treatment. The doctor says…he's got six months to live. You're the last chance that I've got to save the boy."

"Brain tumors are tricky, even for our experts. The price for this kind of treatment isn't cheap, but it's cheaper than what big pharma currently charges."

"How much?"

"$2,000."

"I…I can do that. That's amazing. And affordable."

"You'll have to provide a 50% deposit up front and fill out some paperwork, including a binding non-disclosure agreement and a waiver of liability should the treatment…not work the way it should."

"Dad…this is crazy. You're going to let these people shoot an arrow at my head? What if it works but I'm retarded for the rest of my life?"

"Let me reassure you…Frank…that the practitioners of the Ted Nugent Philosophy of Medicine receive the very best training from masters of Zen archery and from doctors who studied at John Hopkins and Harvard. Our boards are more rigorous than what the state requires. Our success rate has been 65% and climbing. We're not licensed and accredited yet, but with enough data, we should receive approval by no later than the end of the third quarter of this year. You've tried everything else, young man. What do you have to lose?"

"So I have a 35% chance of dying? This is insane. Dad, let's go."

Dr. Harington's phone rings. "Hang on a second." He picks up the receiver. "He's here? Send him right in." Three men in white coats walk in Dr. Harington's office, bows pulled back, aiming at Leopold and Timmy. "You two are terrible liars."

"And what…are we lying about?" Leopold asks.

"Drop the fake American accent, Mr. Franz, or do you prefer Leopold?" Dr. Harington rips the cardigan off of Leopold. "Roll up your sleeves, please?" Leopold rolls up the sleeves on his shirt, revealing a variety of tattoos on his arms. "You couldn't make up a better German name than Gunther Merkel? I'm disappointed in you, and in you, Timmy Hightower." Dr. Harington removes the New Jersey Devils cap, revealing Timmy's blonde buzz cut. He wipes the bags from beneath Timmy's eyes with his thumb.

"How did you know?"

"As you watched the 'testimonial', we were able to bug your phone's operating system, tracking your movements through that instead of the tail we originally had put on you. However, based on your profile, we weren't expecting such clumsiness in gaining access into the school."

"Elias…"

"That's Dr. Harington to you, boy."

"Elias, are you sure you knew where I was the entire time?"

Elias slaps Timmy across the face. "I said that's Dr. Harington to you, boy."

Timmy wipes the blood from the corner of his mouth. "Fine. Dr. Harington, are you sure knew where I was all this time?"

"Yes, why?" Gas seeps into Dr. Harington's office. The doctors/archers and Dr. Harington gag and cry. "Shoot them! Shoot them now!" Leopold drops to the floor, removes the two throwing knives taped on his shoulders, throws them at the doctor/archer to the left and right of him. He sweeps the legs out of the third one. Dr. Harington runs out of his office.

"I got these three…Timmy. Go get Elias."

Timmy jumps out of his wheelchair and runs after Dr. Harington. An arrow grazes his t-shirt.

"That was a warning. Come after me, boy, and the next one will be…" A marble slaps Elias' right eye. He holds his bow hand over it, turns and flees. Timmy sprints, then jumps. Timmy and his right foot slam into

Dr. Harington's back, sending him crashing to the floor. Timmy stands with his foot between Dr. Harington's shoulder blades, aiming his slingshot at the back of the doctor's head.

"You're not the only one who's a good shot."

Three SWAT team members emerge through the teary mist, dragging Dr. Harington and Timmy out to fresh air.

* * *

"That was close, Timmy, too close for comfort." Chief Donaldson leans against his police car, puffing his pipe.

"If it wasn't for Leopold scaring off the first tail, and for switching out my SIM card after it was bugged, we couldn't have pulled this off." Timmy reaches into his shirt, pulls out an activated Bluetooth earpiece, and throws it to Chief Donaldson. "Please thank Officer O'Leary for shadowing my movements these last few days to keep Elias's people off my tail."

"I will, Timmy. I don't think we can get them on the Bishop case, though. It's alternative medicine and he agreed to undergo their treatment. If they could afford a private investigator to dig up dirt on you and Leopold and create sophisticated tracking viruses to plant in cell phones, then they probably have an excellent legal team that could keep the Bishop case locked up in court for years."

"Uncle Leo and I signed no such paperwork. Once they found out who we are, it became attempted murder, two counts. I'm 100% sure they'll go to jail for a long time."

* * *

"Your father…has a strange sense of humor," Leopold says, holding the signature Taco Dog bright yellow fire hydrant shaped cup full of cherry cola.

"How?"

"That last case…people being treated with arrows… like me treating illness…with my knives."

Timmy swallows a bit of the jalapeno, ghost pepper, kimchi salsa inside the Smaug Dog, chases it with a kamikaze of lime soda, vanilla cola, and Jolt. "Humans are so desperate to hold onto their mortality, they'll try anything. My father keeps them good and scared because he needs them to die and from that fear, they create things like Scientology, crystal healing, yoga, acupuncture, things they think will stave off death if they practice them, believe in them hard enough. If they knew the truth, knew of the broken promise that awaits them after they die…until then, my father will continue doing everything he can to make sure they keep missing the mark."

Draining Chutes, Ladders

The glass breaks against Timmy's right shoulder, the shards showering him as he sails over the windowsill, into the living room. He pulls the slingshot out of his back pocket, loads it with a piece of glass.

"Breaking and entering and attempting second degree murder, Timmy Hightower? My my, what happened to the boy who believed in due process?" The light from the lamp on the end table was not strong enough to catch the face of all the questions.

*   *   *

Blood stains Leopold Franz's face and chest after the fourth shower; preschool turned into a mobile. Him and Chief Donaldson tried holding Timmy back from the walking the scene.

"This…why this?" Leopold asks the running

showerhead. The water beneath his feet collects, spurting up from the drain, forming his father's face down to the half smile running down his right cheek.

"Because I could."

*　*　*

"If you were human, it would be murder," the rubber creaks as Timmy keeps the sling taut, aiming at the half silhouette.

"You will become your father by doing this."

Timmy howls as the knife sinks into his hand, the piece of glass flying wildly from the slingshot. The half silhouette screams after two knives pierce it. Timmy rolls on his back, looks up at Leopold.

"Why? Why didn't you let me do it?"

"Monsters…aren't born. Moments like this…make them."

From the Hips

Timmy Hightower crouches over the body, its eyes and mouth weeping vinyl.

"Whatever was used to do this is gone," Chief Donaldson puffs on his pipe while leaning against the empty record shelf. "Randall had a very unique collection. It's too hot for the usual fences."

"Who would have motive to do this to him?"

"Ex-wife maybe? Jealous record collector? I just show you…"

"…the bodies. I have to be the one to follow the leads. I know."

"Speaking of bodies, where's your uncle?"

"Painting the town red, as you'd say. I mean that figuratively, of course."

"Leopold Franz is out at night? Having fun? I didn't think that was possible."

Timmy straightens himself up, turns and faces Chief Donaldson. "In order for Uncle Leo to truly reform, he has to reconnect with humanity. Love can do just that. Or some really good sex."

Chief Donaldson's pipe drops out of his mouth, his jaw unhinging. "Um…I thought…"

"Chief, I was married, despite what you may have read. I never required my followers to be celibate, either. My father, however, believes if his followers aren't getting laid, then they use that pent up sexual energy to serve his purpose. The means behind an end don't really matter to him, as long as he gets what he wants."

"I don't think Leopold knows how to talk to a woman, let alone how to hold a conversation. Who is he out with?"

"Does the name James Decatur ring a bell?"

* * *

Chief Donaldson settles into the couch in Timmy's basement crime lab, watching Timmy drag and drop crime scene photos across the large, flat screen monitor.

"Don't you have other cases to work?" Timmy asks.

"I'm merely an administrator. The last time I solved a case was five years ago. I've always wanted to see how he worked. What is he having you do, anyway?"

"Timmy's instincts are telling me there's a pattern

here." He points at the photo of a woman choking on stamped envelopes. "Carleen Clavin, rare stamp collector. The estimated value of the stamps on one of those envelopes was $20,000. The rest of her collection went missing." Timmy clicks on the mouse to bring another photo to the forefront: wrists and throats slit with tiny, jagged incisions. "Edwin Denson, three-time *Magic: The Gathering* national champion. The estimated value of the deck used as murder weapon was a grand. The rest of his collection, gone." Timmy clicks on the mouse to bring the man weeping and drooling vinyl up on the screen. "And now, Randall Fringston. The part of his collection used to kill him was estimated at $5,000 and the rest is gone."

"We have someone who likes to kill collectors with their own collections and take the rest?"

"That's part of it. I did a little more digging." Timmy presses a few keys on his keyboard, bringing up three official-looking documents. "Each one is divorced, the reasons for the divorce attributed to their obsessions regarding their collections as the deciding factor."

"Wow. What next?"

"Tomorrow, after school, we go to Sandiego's and have a chat with the owner."

"We? Leopold's gonna be back late. He should recovered by the time you get out of school."

"Leopold is off this case. He needs some time to himself. And since all you do is administrate…"

"Wait a minute, Timmy. I need to clear this with your father."

"I already did. Meet me at Sandiego's tomorrow. Plain clothed."

* * *

Timmy threads the bike lock through the spokes of the back wheel of his BMX bike, around the tree, through the spokes of the front wheel, connecting the lock. He notices Chief Donaldson across the street in front of Sandiego's wearing a white polo shirt and light khaki pants, puffing his pipe. "That's your idea of plain clothed?" Timmy yells, as he walks toward Chief Donaldson.

"Yeah, so? Were you expecting me in a suit and tie, oiled shoulder holster hidden beneath my sport coat?"

Timmy stops in front of Chief Donaldson, looks him over. "Uh, yeah."

"This is your investigation, Timmy. I'm merely here to assist and protect you outside of my official capacity as the Chief of Police. While I am operating as your protector, I'm going to be comfortable and before you ask…" Chief Donaldson reaches into his left pocket, pulling out a .38 Special. "…yes, I'm carrying."

"Aren't you afraid that will go off in your pocket?"

"Pocket's cut out, letting me draw from a holster strapped to my thigh." Chief Donaldson puts the .38 back into his pocket. Timmy notices the outline of the gun bulging through Donaldson's khakis after he holsters it.

"Yeah, incompetent gun owner is a good cover for you," Timmy says as he opens the door. Timmy and Chief Donaldson watch a string tied to the doorknob inside pull the trigger of a crossbow balanced on a rack. The bolt skewers through the hood cinched on the man's head tied to a chair behind one of the glass cases. Chief Donaldson runs across the room, takes out a pocketknife, and cuts the hood around the arrow sticking through the body's right eye.

"Timmy, meet Santiago Sandiego. How does it feel to kill a man?"

Timmy runs out of Sandiego's, vomiting onto the curb.

*   *   *

Timmy sits on the back of the ambulance, blanket draped around his shoulders. He stares at the Sandiego's front door. Chief Donaldson snaps his fingers in front of Timmy's face until the boy's eyes flutter and look up.

"Ever heard of a Scorpio?" Donaldson asks.

"A what?"

"That's what killed Sandiego. It was an artillery weapon used by the Romans. Sandiego's specialty was ancient weapons and only that part of the store is gone."

"Divorced?"

"Yup. Because of the money he spent collecting these

weapons."

Timmy slides off the back of the ambulance, letting the blanket fall from his shoulders into the street. He walks over to his bike, kneels, and begins unlocking the bike lock.

"This wasn't your fault, Tim," Chief Donaldson yells as he closes the distance between himself and Timmy. "How could you have known this was going to happen?"

"I should have been more careful," Timmy replies into the sidewalk. "Timmy's supposed to be more careful."

Chief Donaldson gently places a hand on Timmy's shoulder. "Timmy's never dealt with cases like this. Take the night off."

"I can't. I have a case to solve." Timmy wraps the chain around the bike's frame, snaps it shut. He jumps on, pedaling furiously away from the crime scene.

* * *

Chief Donaldson shuts the door behind him, turns on the faucet, twiddling the knobs until the water is slightly warm. "We need to talk."

"We have nothing to talk about," the running water hisses.

"Yes, we do. I didn't sign up for allowing a 12-year-old boy to accidentally kill someone."

"You know he's not a boy."

"I know he's not, but Timmy is. Whatever allows him

to use Timmy's skills and abilities has to be getting back to him wherever you're keeping him. When you're done with his body, his mind will have to cope with all that has happened."

"I have that covered, Craig, as I have everything covered. Where's your faith?"

"Not in you."

The faucet twists until the mouth aims at Chief Donaldson, the knobs twisting clockwise until they crack. The water slams into the right side of Chief Donaldson's ribcage, pinning him against the bathroom door.

"This is a warning. I can find someone to replace you easily. Remember that." The water trickles to a stop.

Chief Donaldson clutches his ribs, heaving.

* * *

Timmy ducks under the police tape, opens the front door of Sandiego's, his hand encased in a questionably clean tube sock. Timmy removes the sock, takes a flashlight out of his backpack, and turns it on. He shines the light on the wall across the room, stares at the faded crimson blotch. Broken glass cracks with each step he takes. Timmy stops in front of one of the broken cases, taking inventory of the knives and swords.

"I'm surprised you came back." Timmy turns, facing a shadow with glowing green eyes. The flashlight dims in Timmy's hands. "Why didn't you believe Chief

Donaldson when he said only the weapons were stolen?"

"I needed to see if he missed something. Donaldson and his crew always miss something."

"Dear boy, your haste is going to cost you."

Timmy throws the dying flashlight at the shadow, running toward it at the same time. He drives his shoulder through the shadow's shins, sending it crashing to the floor. Timmy runs outside, then turns. He stands in front of Sandiego's, bouncing on the balls of his feet, fists clenched in a fighting stance.

"Let's see how you do out here."

"Another time." A grenade breaks through the front door's glass pane. Timmy sprints across the street, ducking beneath the nearest car. The grenade settles to a stop on a sewer grate, waiting.

*　*　*

"I said take the night off, Tim." Chief Donaldson winces as he takes a slow drag off his pipe.

"A man died, Chief. A man died by my hands. I won't stand for it."

"Haven't people died because of you already?"

Timmy crosses his arms; his eyebrows slant. "Really, you are going to ask me that here?"

"Alright, fair enough. There weren't any prints on the practice grenade your attacker threw out of Sandiego's. However, whatever you did finally gave us something we can use to track this bastard." Chief Donaldson takes an evidence bag off the roof of his car and hands it to Timmy. Timmy holds it up, watching the tooth slide down inside, following a thin trail of blood.

"Our suspect also may have a limp." Timmy hands the evidence bag back to Chief Donaldson. "If our suspect is smart, they'll avoid the ER or emergency dentists to fix either one of their problems."

"Could you tell the gender of the suspect?"

"It was too dark. I also couldn't tell based on the voice. They changed their voice deliberately to make it harder to figure them out."

"If our suspect profiled you well enough to figure you'd double back to look at the crime scene, they might be waiting for you at home. I can have a couple of officers take you home and accompany you inside."

"I don't think they'll be a need but I will. For your sake."

* * *

The officers standing on each side of Timmy collapse. Timmy crouches, looks at the tranquilizer darts sticking in their necks. A dove lands on one of the officer's chests.

"It's not safe here," the dove coos. "Get back to the station and work from there."

Timmy stands, turns, looks around. "Who is doing this?"

"I'm not even supposed to be warning you. Get back

to the station." Timmy watches the dove fly towards the moon.

*   *   *

"Timmy…what are you…"

Timmy comes around Chief Donaldson's desk, presses a couple of keys on Donaldson's keyboard. Timmy's basement/crime lab comes up on the monitor.

"I was told by a reliable source my house wasn't safe." Timmy moves the mouse to the left, the view of the screen changing to focus on the door leading back upstairs, then moves the mouse to the right, scanning the lab. "I don't see anything. It might be on the other side of the door. Or somewhere else in the house."

"Where are the officers I sent along to escort you?"

"Dreaming, thanks to a couple of well-placed tranquilizer darts. Peter made sure they wouldn't walk into a death trap."

"Peter?"

"You might know him as the gatekeeper. He normally operates unseen on my father's behalf. If Peter's stepping in to help, this is really bad."

"I can get the bomb squad out to your house to take a look."

Timmy opens a new window on the screen, enters a command. He pushes the keyboard back, walks out of Donaldson's office. Chief Donaldson takes the gun from his front desk drawer, holsters it, and runs after Timmy.

* * *

Timmy stares at the front door. He doesn't turn when Chief Donaldson's car parks against the curb, the engine quieting down.

"Tim, what are you doing?" Chief Donaldson says as he gets out of the car.

"Our suspect won't expect me to go through the front door." Timmy takes two steps before Chief Donaldson grips Timmy's right shoulder, pulling him back.

"You are going to get Timmy killed."

"Give me your phone?" Timmy turns, holding out his hand.

"What does my phone have to do with anything?"

"Just give it to me, Chief." Chief Donaldson fishes through his pockets, hands Timmy the cobalt blue encased iPhone. Timmy presses a couple of buttons on the phone, bringing up a photo of the man weeping vinyl, handing the iPhone back to Chief Donaldson. "What's missing on the body?"

Chief Donaldson squints. "The...left ear."

"Look at the next one." Chief Donaldson thumbs to a photo of a woman choking on stamped envelopes. "What do you see?"

"Blood...blood is coming out the sides of her mouth."

"Our collector killer isn't just killing collectors with the things they love. Our collector killer is also collecting body parts that focused on what senses were most needed to be good at collecting what they did."

"They're after Leopold's knives, then. The killer keeps coming after you, hoping Leopold steps up to them."

"Leopold hasn't allowed a collection to drive away someone he loves. Timmy has."

"The newspaper clippings, the mementos encased in Lucite in Timmy's basement crime lab. That's what they're after."

"And Timmy's right leg."

Chief Donaldson walks to the trunk and opens it. He hands Timmy a set of yellow plastic earmuffs, before pulling out a riot gun and a set of yellow plastic earmuffs, placing it on his head. "Put them on." Chief Donaldson watches Timmy put on the earmuffs before taking a few steps towards Timmy's house, pumps the riot gun, firing canisters through the front windows. The earmuffs muffle the shrill howl coming from inside, a black figure jumping through what's left of one of the front windows, writhing on the ground, covering their ears. Chief Donaldson walks up to the writhing figure, kicks its jaw to make it stop. Timmy kneels, removes the night vision goggles from the figure. Chief Donaldson takes the flashlight from his belt, shines it on the figure's face, her green eyes rolling back, blood trickling from her ears. Timmy steps back, mouth agape.

* * *

"I'm…going to lock my knives up better." Leopold sits at the dining room table, cleaning his throwing knives.

"I'm going…to have to practice with these…to make sure they're properly balanced. We'll need…to improve the security system, too."

"Chief Donaldson saved my life. If I would have gone in through the basement window or the front door, I would have bled out on the floor. Her attack on me at Sandiego's after dark was part of her whole misdirection strategy to turn our house into a death trap. She knew that when I finished what she started, it would unnerve me."

"You and her younger sister, Marie…were together for two years. She used…to babysit you. I hope she's the last Swanson…to come after you or else…we'll be dealing with more…*Home Alone* guerrilla style attacks."

"*Home Alone?*"

"Never…mind."

We're Not in Kansas Anymore

1.

"We found this in the ruins." Chief Donaldson hands Timmy Hightower an evidence bag with a charred plastic baby, blackened blonde hair, blue eyes, its stomach blown open.

"Let me guess…"

"Yeah. Work fast. Your father's not a fan of this kind of thing."

2.

Leopold Franz flips backwards. Three knives quiver in its trunk as Leopold lands on his feet.

"Are you ok, Leo?" Timmy sips on his kamikaze mix of soda in his bright yellow Taco Dog fire hydrant cup.

"No." Two more knives disappear from his vest, landing between the knives quivering in the tree trunk.

3.

The delivery driver rubbed his wrist before walking into Captain Power Play, leaving the package at the base of the *Mappy-Land* arcade cabinet.

4.

"What's the symbolism of *Mappy-Land*?" Timmy sits in front of his computer.

"Mappy…land?" The couch creaks as Leopold adjusts. "I'm…"

"You don't know do you? You normally give me shit for not knowing pop culture references."

"Did you just…curse?"

"Yeah. Shit."

5.

"Peter, what's wrong?"

"These children…their energy…Timmy's bonds are loosening."

"What?"

"If Timmy awakens, he could finally take back his

body and send your son back here."

"We can't have that. We're not ready."

6.

The volume of Mappy's head prevents him from jumping any higher than one pica. He powers through his hydrocephalus to collect enough cheese to mack on the eventual love of his life.

7.

"In order for Mappy to progress through the game, he has to collect cheese, then wedding rings, then Christmas trees, and finally baseballs," Timmy rubs his chin.

"Why…blow up an arcade?"

"Most arcades now take tokens or swipe cards but Captain Power Play still uses quarters. And quarters are a result of paper money, which is also called…"

"…cheese."

8.

Rings, bracelets, watches, charms, glass flew throughout the building. One person was found with diamonds in his throat.

9.

"The bodies keep coming too quick, sir. I can't keep

up."

"Peter, do what you must. Enlist additional help if you have to. Are the containment suits charged?"

"Yes."

"Then get more help."

10.

"What are you doing here?" The dove perches on the handlebars of Timmy Hightower's BMX bike.

"I need you to work faster."

"That's not the only reason why you're down here are you?"

"Since when do I need to explain myself."

11.

"Damn it, Timmy, that's two buildings now blown up in two days." Chief Donaldson puffs his pipe angrily.

"We have two more chances to catch him."

"What are you talking about?"

Timmy throws the *Mappy-Land* cartridge on Chief Donaldson's desk. "Got a Nintendo?"

12.

Once there was a boy who used *Mappy-Land* as the centerpiece of his fifth grade birthday party, but turned down the *Mappy-Land* music so everyone could better hear the New Kids On The Block album on repeat in the tape deck. It took another 15 years before that boy finally got his first kiss.

13.

The delivery driver uppercuts and roundhouse kicks his shadow. He takes the brown towel from a nearby chair, wipes the sweat off his face. "I'm almost there," he huffs. "I'm almost there."

14.

"It's July. There's nothing Christmas related…in July."

"Yes, there's nothing Christmas related exactly, Leo, but our bomber has a flexible interpretation." Timmy bites into the Ghost Face Killer taco, the snap of the dog and its ghost pepper filling souring his face.

"Hello, Timmy." A fist cracks against Leopold's jaw.

15.

Timmy's eyes flutter. The rope chaffs against his wrist as he struggles to get free.

"Good to see you awake, Timmy." A man in a powder blue hat, polo shirt, and black shorts places a package on Timmy's lap. "I was afraid you would miss this."

"I have nothing to do with Christmas."

"Yes, you do." The man waves his left hand over his

right wrist, revealing a bronze bracelet. "Long time, no see."

16.

Leopold rubs his jaw, brings himself to his feet. A dove lands on the table next to him.

"Get yourself together, Leo," the dove coos. "We have a problem."

"Where's…where's Timmy?"

"Adam has him."

17.

"This won't free her," Timmy yells.

"But I thought you wanted to go home."

"On my terms, not yours."

"He'll be too overwhelmed to notice, but I guess you've been too busy to follow how things have escalated in Syria."

18.

Leopold grips the steering wheel of his cobalt blue El Camino when a black van pulls up next to him, opens the side door. He ignores the muzzle flash, the hail of bullets shattering the glass as he cuts into the black van's lane.

19.

Mappy-Land didn't allow its police force to carry any weapons, which explained the police force's high attrition and low enrollment numbers in its academy.

20.

Leopold holds the knife to the gunman's throat. The driver gurgles.

"Where's…Timmy?"

A dove lands on the van's roof. "They won't tell you anything. This is just a distraction. Get back on the road."

"Where's…Timmy?" The knife's edge presses into the gunman's throat.

21.

"Eve, where are you?"

A man emerges from behind the rocks, armor covered in blood. "I'm…" An arrow punctures his throat.

22.

"I know she's up there somewhere, safe. I've got a man on the inside who will get what I need and we'll be together again." Adam steps back, pulls out his cellphone. "I think ten minutes should be enough for me to get out of the building and away from the blast zone."

"He's going to find you."

"Your father or Leopold? I've taken care of them both."

23.

The bullet goes through the dove's belly, a knife goes into the gunman's hand.

"Leopold…finish it."

Leopold takes the dove's neck between his finger and thumb.

24.

"Peter." Peter looks over at the diver's suit clanging towards him.

"Timmy?"

"Who have you freed to help out with the volume that might have motive to help Adam get the containment unit holding Eve?"

25.

After all the baseballs are collected, *Mappy-Land* resets itself to where you collect cheese. Some theorists would say this reflects the cycle of death and rebirth. Other theorists would say Mappy got divorced and is wooing another lady using repetitive techniques. People with lives would say it's just a video game.

26.

Timmy closes his eyes, watches two early Twentieth Century diving suits fight.

27.

"Enough," the air shouts. "What is Timmy doing awake, Peter?"

"He...found who was working with Adam...down there."

One of the diving suits spontaneously vaporizes, the other collapses.

"Take Timmy back to his room. It's time we finish this."

28.

The handle of a knife cracks against Adam's jaw. Leopold looks down at the cellphone, sees four minutes ticking down.

29.

"Leopold won't get to him in four minutes. What will you do?"

"Peter...it's time to put all this extra energy to good use."

30.

The handle of a knife cracks against the delivery driver's jaw, collapsing in front of Captain Power Play. Leopold cuts the box open, diffuses the bomb.

"How…" the delivery driver mutters before passing out. Leopold waves his hand over the delivery driver's right wrist. Nothing appears. Leopold looks up.

"Where…is it?"

Philadelphia

"What the Hell happened to you?" Chief Donaldson's pipe dangles from his lips.

"I got elbowed off a moped and landed really hard on my right shoulder." Timmy Hightower squirms, adjusting the sling suspending his right forearm. "I almost had him. Almost."

"Who?"

"Ronald Ewe, the guy who's shearing blonde men and wearing their skin."

"FBI's on that now. Seems he did that to Congressman Carlo's lover."

"He's never pulled me from a case before."

"Well, his priorities have changed." Chief Donaldson steps aside. Timmy sees two smoldering bodies slumped in the alley. Chief Donaldson hands Timmy an evidence bag. "We found this in what we think used to be the man's right pocket. We're surprised it didn't melt." Timmy stares at the charred, metallic snake.

"What happened?"

"Dinner, lightning."

"My father could figure this out on his own. He sees everything."

"He can't see this and he needs to know why."

* * *

"How long...has it been since you broke something?" Leopold sharpens one of his throwing knives, looking at the edge in the light.

"When I was seven, I was fooling around with some friends on a roof and I fell. I woke up a few hours later in bed, my mom and stepfather hovering over me. I wasn't broken long." Timmy winces as he adjusts his arm in the sling. "I don't know if I can deal with this thing for eight weeks."

"At least...you'll have to finally let me do my job...as your guardian."

"I guess so." Timmy drags the keyboard to the edge of the desk, presses a few keys. "So we have John Bull and Gina Drang, ages 28 and 25. Witnesses say they met outside of the restaurant, had drinks and appetizers, a good time. Most likely, they decided to take it to they alley and then zzzt."

"How...did they meet?"

"John just moved here from Georgia after his wife died. He was a call center trainer at a collections agency. Gina was a law clerk so it wasn't at work. According to Gina's best friend, she mentioned she was meeting a guy from a dating site. It was her first date since...her husband died."

"That...seems a little weird."

"Yeah." Timmy presses a couple of keys, pulls up obituaries. "John's wife died when she ran out of air while underwater cave diving. Gina's husband..."

"Yes?"

Timmy swivels his office chair to face Leopold. "Gina's husband was struck by lightning."

* * *

Timmy and Leopold stare at the blackened brick in the alley, protected by police tape. "Based on where the strike occurred, the pattern of the burn, it looks like the lightning bolt came from..." Timmy turns around to look at the building behind them "...the ninth or tenth floor here."

"The guy paid cash when he rented the space," Sal Hanson says as he unlocks the door to Suite 1031. "He paid for a month."

"Did he say what his name was," asks Timmy.

"Ben Edison."

"Are...you kidding me?" Leopold asks.

Sal, Timmy, and Leopold walk into the suite. "Goddamn it, he better have given me enough to cover this." Sal points to the wood covering the hole in the plate glass window. Timmy walks around and notices three circular indentations in the carpet.

"This is where he fired from, for sure."

"What," asks Leopold.

"A lightning cannon?"

*   *   *

"Someone managed to sew a lightning rod into John's shirt." Timmy stares at the report. "Leopold, they met online, right?"

"Yes."

"Gina's sister didn't say what site it was though."

"She...didn't know. She just said Gina met John online."

"Ok. So Gina and John both lost their spouses tragically. However, they died like Gina's husband." Timmy turns to the computer, types 'widows + dating' into the search engine. Timmy clicks on a link to "Six Feet Undercovers," prompting Dave Matthews to start howling about digging shallow graves to feel the rain.

*   *   *

"I..." Raymond R. Charmaigne eases back in his leather office chair, folding his hands, staring into the web cam. "...I'm stunned about their deaths. You think my site has something to do with it, Mr. Hightower?"

"Mr. Charmaigne, I do. Gina's husband died here, so there's a possibility that the killer read about how he died in the paper but this was specific. The killer had a lighting rod sewn into John's shirt. He knew John was going out on a date, where he was going, and what his game plan was prior to going on the date."

"We do encourage our users to discuss their dating plans with their potential partners through our secure instant messaging and e-mail system."

"Are you sure it's secure?"

"Based on what you're telling me, I'm not so sure now."

"I need your security team to take a look at their account history, at any possible breaches. Would you be willing to do that?"

"Absolutely. Can you assure me discretion about this matter in the event our site was hacked?"

"Yes. When will you know?"

"Give me 48 hours."

Timmy's cellphone vibrates. He flips it open and reads the text message. "Mr. Charmaigne, try to make it 24."

* * *

Timmy and Leopold watch the smoke bellow from the car, fire hoses dousing the ruined frame.

A black sedan parks next to Chief Donaldson's police car. A man in a leather jacket, black Polo shirt, and jeans steps out of the car, walks toward Chief Donaldson. "What happened here?"

"Who are…" Chief Donaldson stops when he sees the U.S. Marshal's badge around the man's neck.

"Edward Dixon, U.S. Marshals."

"Chief Craig Donaldson." His offered hand hangs in the air.

"One of the women in the car was Beth Winston. She was in the Witness Protection Program." Edward looks at Timmy and Leopold. "Who are these two and what are they doing here?"

"The boy is a consultant we use from time to time on certain cases. The man with him is his uncle and guardian. This incident is possibly part of an active case he's helping with."

"You consult with children on cases?"

"It's Timmy Hightower."

"Look, if this involved a treasure map or a lost artifact or someone wearing a monster costume to scare people away from a landmark, then yeah, a boy detective would be the best person to consult. A federally protected witness was murdered."

"We don't know that yet. There could have been something wrong with the car."

"Cars don't just blow up. What kind of police chief are you?"

"I…won't answer that," Leopold says.

"You two need to leave. Now!" Edward yells at Leopold and Timmy. "This case is under my jurisdiction now. There's nothing you can do about it, Chief."

"Yeah, I guess you're right about that."

*   *   *

"Beth Winston, a.k.a. Rachel Wadwall was out on a date with Wendy Yasmain. Beth's husband was killed by a car bomb. Wendy's partner died in a car accident with a drunk driver. They met on Six Feet Undercovers."

"What…are you thinking?" Leopold spins a throwing knife between his fingers.

"Someone is targeting users of the site here in town and killing them off in the same way or what appears to be the same way as one of their spouses died. I can't figure out the motive though."

"Maybe…someone thinks reuniting them with who they lost is better than having them coping with…the loss."

"Mary didn't kill herself when I died, Leo. It was hard watching her move on but I knew she had to."

"Didn't…you see her again after she died?"

"It doesn't work like that, Leo. It…" Timmy places his hand over his mouth, closes his eyes for a moment, breathing deeply before opening his eyes. "It doesn't work like that."

Timmy drags the keyboard close to the edge of the desk so his right hand can reach the keys. "Charmaigne granted me admin access to the site. I think I can run a data miner that will help us figure out when the next two people are going out on a date and where."

"We need to be…careful…whoever this is…they are precise. Did you ever find out about how…John's shirt was altered?"

"John's tailor was paid $500 cash to sew it in, no questions. He said the guy's name was David Tesla."

Leopold slaps his forehead. "Really?"

"Is the alias that obvious?"

"Yes. I'm…surprised you haven't tried running the aliases through…Timmy's search programs."

"What other aliases could he use?"

"Westinghouse…is the only other one I could think of. He financed…Tesla. Ben Franklin…discovered electricity. If we are going to really stretch it, Dr. Frankenstein used it…to bring life, but he was fictional."

"Wait." Timmy pushes away the keyboard, moves aside. "Come take a look." Leopold sees Shelley Westinghouse's profile. "Time to pay him a visit."

*   *   *

"Thanks for the lead, kid." Edward Dixon leans against his sedan. Two SWAT vans empty in front of the house. "I know you and Leopold have a habit of being the ones who take the bad guys down but, y'know, federal jurisdiction and all."

"You need to be careful, sir," Timmy says. "He might have wanted us to find him."

"We're always careful." Edward covers his right ear for a moment. "Go!"

Four SWAT team members smash the door open with a battering ram. A lightning bolt strikes one of the SWAT vans, the engine ruptures. Timmy and Leopold take cover behind the nearest tree, screams and the smell of cooking metal and flesh choking the air. After a minute or two of silence, Timmy and Leopold emerge, staring at the aftermath.

"You were right about me wanting to be found," the amplified voice echoes. "It was never about the widows or the widowers. They were just a means to draw you out."

"What are you talking about," Timmy yells, looking around.

"You are no mere boy, Mr. Hightower. You might be in the shell of a child but in you there is so much more. Your bioelectricity is like none I have ever seen. I've studied your case files. How can a 12-year-old boy break a grown man's knee cap with just one kick?"

"Training."

"Perhaps. However, with your build and estimated musculature, it would take three or four well placed kicks even with your training."

"Why don't you show yourself and find out?"

"You are not as effective with a broken shoulder."

"Where is he, Leo?"

"Don't bother whispering, Mr. Hightower. I hear and see all. And, Mr. Franz, it will hurt far worse if you don't keep those knives where they are now." Timmy watches a dart sink into Leopold's neck, then his own. On the ground, Timmy watches the tree trunk open, feels rubbery fingers grip his ankles.

* * *

"Timmy! Time for breakfast." Timmy sits straight up in bed, rubs his eyes. "Timmy! Did you hear me? You're going to be late for school."

"Mom?"

"Wake up, Tim. Rise and shine. Get down here. Now!"

Timmy stares at the scrambled eggs, bacon, and white toast on the black porcelain plate.

"You ok, Tim?" Mary Hightower pours over her legal briefs.

"I…I had a weird dream. You and dad were dead and Uncle Leo was taking care of me and we were solving these really bizarre cases."

Mary puts the brief down, looks at Timmy, holds his right hand. "You can't keep skipping your medication, Tim."

"What medication?"

"What medication? Oh, Tim. Wait until your father is

back from assignment."

"Where's Dad?"

"Some godforsaken part of South America. He's been there for a month now. His handlers tell me he's still alive, thank God. I keep telling him to stop chasing after coke kingpins but he never listens."

"Why…you never…you never complain like this…"

Lightning shoots out of one of the outlets in the kitchen, impaling Mary through her stomach, setting her legal briefs on fire. Timmy jumps away from the table, howling.

* * *

Timmy's fingers tremble on Marie Swanson's waist as the DJ plays The Cure's "Just Like Heaven".

"I always wanted to dance to this song." Marie rests her chin on Timmy's shoulder, bringing them closer. Timmy notices a chaperone wading through the other slow dancing seventh graders.

"Marie…"

"Yes, Tim?"

The chaperone places her hands on Timmy and Marie's shoulder, gently prying them apart. A lightning bolt pierces the roof, striking the chaperone. Timmy, Marie, and other seventh graders nearby wear parts of her.

* * *

Lightning snakes down Timmy's throat as he bites into

the Taco Dog. Lightning strikes in the middle of the groom's side at the chapel, setting Leopold on fire.

* * *

"I will kill you if I have to, Mr. Hightower, and dissect your body to find out the source of your magnificent energy."

Timmy opens his eyes, struggles to turn his head. "You…know…who…who I am."

"You have an old soul, Mr. Hightower, one that grants you vitality and strength unlike any human I have ever seen. Nothing more."

"Why…won't you…say his name?" Timmy runs his tongue over his cracked, dry lips.

"Whose?"

"You…know…who."

"If it is who you think you may be talking about, all of that is mere fiction, men of clay, women of rib, fires, flood. The violence though is a lot of fun."

"Then why won't you…say his name?"

"Mr. Hightower, I know what you are trying to do. As long as I do not say the names or think the names or believe in any of the names, I cannot be seen. Again, I have done my homework on you. It took far less time to break him but…" A black-gloved hand waves a split open bronze bracelet in front of Timmy's face, "… he told me what I needed to know and when he did, I finally gave him what he truly wanted."

"Adam…never wanted death."

"After all I did to him, he begged for it. He broke like all men do. I expect that's where we get it from, the need to break when time calls for us not to be broken. So much for the so-called first man." Timmy hears the flipping of switches, the hum of a generator. "Let's try this again, shall we?"

* * *

"Wake…" Leopold kips up from the ground and holds a knife to Chief Donaldson's throat.

"Chief…" Leopold sheathes the knife in his vest. "…sorry. Force of habit."

Chief Donaldson rubs his throat. "Good to see you've broken at least some of those habits. Where's Timmy?"

"I…don't know. I was hit with…a tranquilizer dart…first."

"Look behind you." Leopold sees disheveled grass and dirt stretching out towards the oak tree in the front yard. "It looks like Timmy was dragged over there." Leopold and Chief Donaldson follow the path until it stops in front of the oak tree.

"I'm surprised…he hasn't caught on to us. He… could hear and see everything that was going on…fried everything but us."

"He must be distracted then." Chief Donaldson looks up to the sky. "A little help here?" The clouds reply "NO."

"What…an asshole." Leopold feels the tree trunk, his hands stumbling onto the hinges, the seam of the door. He unsheathes two knives. "I think…I found our way in."

* * *

Lightning strikes Timmy's back as he falls off the roof of his parents' house. Timmy rides lightning to his baseball game. Timmy pulls out textbooks made of lightning from his locker. Lightning blocks Timmy's jumping roundhouse kick. Timmy finds a body of lightning at the scene laying in a pool of its own electrostatic.

* * *

"Timmy? Timmy?" Timmy wakes up to Chief Donaldson slapping his right cheek, Leopold unstrapping him.

"Where's…Shelly?"

"He…must have escaped when we made our way inside." Leopold lifts Timmy, slumps him over his shoulders. "Let's get you…to the hospital."

"No…hospital. Take me home."

"Tim, we're taking you to a hospital." Chief Donaldson looks around the room.

"No…I need to have…a conversation…with my father. Home, now."

* * *

Timmy sits in the full bathtub, breathing heavily.

Leopold kneels next to Timmy. "Leopold, are you ready?"

"No. What if…"

"The last time we did this, he interfered. He doesn't want me to die."

"I hope…you are right."

Timmy slips beneath the water. Leopold presses down on Timmy's chest, watches the air bubble slowly out of Timmy's mouth, then frantically.

"Timmy? Timmy!"

* * *

"Did Adam get what you needed from him," Peter asks.

"No," the air hisses. "He withstood his greatest efforts."

"What about Timmy?"

"Unaffected. He managed to sever the connection so whatever was done the body; it would not come back to him here. Peter, I'm concerned. The boy's body isn't resisting or rejecting my son. It's adapting, protecting him. If this pattern continues, he could come back here without my assistance or permission."

"Then you need to end this before that happens. You are pushing this experiment of yours to the very brink. You will cost us everything."

"Or it will grant this place, us, new life. Great reward does not come without great risk. Faith, Peter, remember?"

"I have faith. I also have common sense. I don't want my last words to be 'I told you so'."

"Who said you'll have any last words?"

Doing That Little Thing

"Chief, you gotta come see this," Officer Williams yells from the makeshift backstage area.

"When you've seen one coke overdose, you've seen them all," Chief Donaldson yells back. "Let me know when the CSI shows up."

"Sir…" Officer Williams pushes past the blue velvet curtain separating the backstage from the catwalk. "You really need to come see this." Officer Williams parts the curtain. Chief Donaldson sees over Williams' shoulder toned legs on the floor, the calves and knees spattered in blood. He walks through the curtain, looks down.

"That's…"

"Yeah."

Chief Donaldson looks at his watch. "It's not too late to give him a call."

"Who?" Chief Donaldson turns, walks away from the body and Officer Williams. "No, really?"

"Yeah, really."

"This one..."

"Everyone always says whenever a case like this comes up that it's too much for him and every time, he proves them wrong."

"But, Chief..."

"Officer Williams, the fastest way to direct traffic for the rest of your career is to finish that sentence. Is that understood?" Officer Williams nods tentatively. "Finish setting up the perimeter. Now." Officer Williams disappears behind the curtain. Chief Donaldson looks up. "Williams is right. This one might be a bit much. Are you sure you want him to solve it?" A lightning bolt strikes through the giant white tent covering the catwalk, landing at Chief Donaldson's feet. The scorched earth spells "YES".

* * *

"You really had to pull me out of class for this?" Timmy Hightower sat in Chief Donaldson's office, holding a closed manilla folder.

"Ever heard of Rayne LeBlanc?"

"Um..."

"I know you've been down here long enough to actually soak in some of the local culture."

"The teen supermodel, Rayne LeBlanc, the one pretty much every boy in the world has a crush on, Rayne LeBlanc?"

"That one."

"Why?"

"Open the folder."

Timmy opens the manilla folder, stares at the crime scene photos. "…her upper torso was found…flayed…" Timmy looks up at Chief Donaldson. "And the skin?"

"Nowhere to be found."

Timmy closes the folder. "Any leads?"

"She's one of the most famous models on the planet. Her frenemies list could populate our town twelve times over. I don't even know where to begin."

"How's the crime scene?"

"Pretty intact."

"Take me there."

*   *   *

Timmy steps around the neon green tape outline of Rayne LeBlanc's body, noticing how the police took extra care to ensure the tape's legs were as shapely as hers. Officer Williams watches Timmy look around the crime scene.

"Was anything moved other than the body, Officer Williams?"

"No. I did my best to make this place look like all time stopped."

"Find any clues?"

"Didn't you read the file, Timmy?" Timmy stops and stares into Officer Williams.

"The file never tells the whole story, Officer. You of all people should know that."

"I'm not going to have a 12-year-old tell me how to do my job." Officer Williams storms past Timmy. "I'll be waiting out here. Just peek your head out when you're done."

Timmy takes a pair of latex gloves out of his back pocket. He opens the drawer in front of where Rayne sat to have her make-up done. He lifts a jewel case out of the top drawer. The words on the insert beneath say "I'm Too Sexy" printed on lipstick, with the letters "R - S - F" below.

* * *

"Have you heard of this song, Leopold?"

Leopold Franz stops throwing knives across Timmy's crime lab, listens. "I'm...not into...modern music."

"It's catchy. And egotistical. I thought for a moment that Rayne might have been into throwbacks when she walked the catwalk but based on all the video I've watched online, she only walks to upbeat German or French techno."

"You said...it was egotistical. Why?"

Timmy presses a couple of buttons on his keyboard. "The lyrics. 'I'm too sexy for my shirt. Too sexy for my shirt, so sexy it hurts.' No one is that sexy."

"How…was her body found?"

"She was…" Timmy pushes his office chair back, swivels it toward Leopold. "Her upper torso…the skin was missing."

"Do you think…?"

Timmy turns back to the computer, maximizes the browser with the lyrics. "That this is a blueprint?" Timmy's cellphone vibrates on his desk. He picks it up, presses it to his ear.

"I'm sending a squad car to your house. There's something you need to see."

* * *

Timmy and Chief Donaldson stand over a tan, muscular man's body, his feet tied to his neck, the flashes from the paparazzi's camera splashing against their back.

"Get those parasites out of here, now!" Chief Donaldson yells. "These animals…"

"Chief, what happened?"

"A couple stepped out of the club to make out and they stumbled onto him."

"Who was he?"

"Serge Condaana, third sexiest man alive."

"Did you just say 'sexiest'?"

"Yes."

Timmy reaches into his pocket and pulls out a piece of paper. "This club…what music does it play?"

"It's a Donna Summer tribute tonight."

Timmy shoves the paper into Chief Donaldson's hands. "Apparently he was too sexy for this party. There was no way he was disco dancing."

"What's…Timmy, what's going on?"

"When I took a look around at the scene where Rayne was found, I found a CD titled 'I'm Too Sexy'."

"So…Rayne was too sexy for her shirt?"

"And Serge was too sexy for this party."

"But if these lyrics establish a pattern, then there would have to have been more deaths than these two."

"Chief, who knows best how to track the movements of any famous person?" Chief Donaldson looks over his shoulder at the wall of flashing lights and questions.

"I'm going to call Interpol to see what leads I can get. Based on…" An explosion cuts off Donaldson. The paparazzi stop and run toward the chaos.

"Chief, what kind of car did Serge drive?"

"A hand polished silver Bentley."

"Would you give the lyrics back please?" Chief Donaldson hands the page back to Timmy. "It looks like, most likely, someone is going to be too sexy for their hat. My best guess is that the next victim will be scalped or beheaded, probably a prominent hair model."

"I'll get back to the station right away. It's morning in Europe right now. I'll call you as soon as I find out what's going on."

* * *

"Johan…are you ready with my goat milk conditioner? You know how I must have it to ensure my hair looks its very best."

"Oh, don't worry," the shadow whispers placing a gloved hand on the shoulder of the person sitting in the barber's chair. "You'll look your…" The gloved hand spins the chair around revealing a boy in a New York Mets cap holding a digital recorder.

"Hello, Mr. Towns," Timmy says. The man takes a step back.

"How did you…"

"Your girlfriend left you three years ago because of your career as a paparazzo. You were deported out of Italy last year for your behavior at Fashion Week, charged with possession with intent to sell in Manhattan three months ago, skipped out on bail. My theory is that you are killing all of these models to get your girlfriend back in your arms."

"Who…you won't stop me, you little…"

Timmy jumps on top of the barber's chair and then at Mr. Towns, spinning in mid air. The instep of Timmy's right foot connects with Mr. Towns' jaw, his head and neck twisting to the right. Timmy sweeps Mr. Towns' legs from beneath him, stomps his crotch for good measure. Leopold jumps out of the closet, two throwing knives in hand.

"You got him," Leopold asks.

"Yeah, Uncle Leo, I got him." Timmy pants, takes off his hat to wipe his brow. "Where he's going, he'll have plenty of time to shake that little tush on the catwalk."

Wearing Black & Blue

Timmy Hightower dodges to the left, narrowly avoiding Brent Lancaster's jumping axe kick. Brent's right forearm stops Timmy's roundhouse kick.

"All this crime solving's made you soft, man." Brent bounces on the balls of his feet.

"Maybe." Timmy sops up the sweat from his brow with the sleeve of his uniform. "Maybe, I'm just getting warmed up." Brent catches Timmy's left jab, throwing him over his shoulder. Brent sits on Timmy's chest, right fist cocked and shaking.

"You gonna give?"

"Tell me about Stan Mangum," Timmy pants.

"Stan?" Brent loosens his fist. "What about…Stan?"

* * *

Timmy stood in the opening connecting the boys locker room to the shower as crime scene investigators cataloged the dents in the lockers, the broken shower tile, the bruises and contusions on the body drowning beneath the sobbing shower head. A hand on his shoulder brought him from the scene.

"Tim, thanks for coming." Timmy noticed Chief Donaldson's pipe in his left pocket, the puffiness of his eyes.

"This is a pretty good reason to drag me out of first period. I'm surprised Principal Jordan was able to keep this quiet."

"The custodian who lives on the property called it in early this morning. Jordan's cleaning things up on his end."

"What do you think happened?"

"A natural disaster. Or a brawl. I'm not sure."

"Let me guess. My father wants me to take this one."

"Actually, no. I'm asking you to take it."

"What's he gonna say about that?"

"Don't care. I need you more than he does. My youngest looking undercover might pass as an eighth grader who's been held back six years in a row. Possible, but not believable. That's why *21 Jump Street* was plausible with high school students."

"*21 Jump...*"

"Don't worry about it. I forget who I'm talking to.

Anyway, will you do this, for me?"

Timmy watched over Chief Donaldson's shoulder a dove perched on the windowsill above the lockers, pecking at the pane furiously. "You know what my father can do to you, right?"

"Yeah."

"How do you know the victim?"

"He's…the son of an old friend. Please, Tim, you're the only one with the access that I can trust to handle this. Please?"

* * *

Timmy sifted through the crime scene photos, spreading them out on the kitchen table. He stood over them and stared.

"Working…up here now?" Leopold held a plate beneath the running faucet while scrubbing the ketchup stains from the rim.

"It's not that kind of case."

Leopold turned off the faucet, walked over to the kitchen table. "These…aren't as gruesome as usual. Has your father…gone soft?"

"This isn't from him. I took this one as a favor for Chief Donaldson."

"What…about your father?"

"My father won't do anything to me." Timmy picked up the magnifying glass, twirled it through his fingers.

"Chief said that the boy was the son of an old friend. I didn't think the Chief had friends."

"There…there is one person I can think of. It's too soon…to talk to her."

"Who?"

"Colleen Mangum. Her last name…used to be Newson."

"Hmmm. That solves that mystery." Timmy placed the magnifying glass in front of his right eye and looked above the dented lockers at the limp video camera. "Why does the boys' locker room have a video camera in it?"

* * *

Coach Reinhelm stared at the photo, then above the lockers, then back at the photo. "What camera? There's not one up there."

"The one in the photo. You don't recall ever seeing this camera before?" Timmy ran his fingers through his hair.

"Do I look like a pervert to you?"

"I just want to know about the camera."

"And I asked you, do I look like a pervert to you?"

Timmy listened to the fluttering of the police tape in the air conditioning, Reinhelm's angry breathing.

* * *

"Any luck finding footage of last night?" Principal Jordan looked up at Timmy leaning against the frame of the door to his office. Jordan's right hand reached for his Windsor knot, straightening the Parker Lewis Middle School crimson power tie.

"There's a gap between three and four in the morning. There weren't any power outages, though."

"Is there a way to remotely access the cameras?"

"It's a closed circuit. Someone would had to have been on school grounds to shut the cameras outside of the boys' locker room on both sides."

Timmy laid the photo of the ruined locker room and a magnifying glass on Principal Jordan's desk. "Do you recall having a camera installed inside the boys locker room?"

Principal Jordan picked up the magnifying glass, closed his left eye, squinted his right. "That's…that's a camera alright. Why would I do something like that?"

"I know you've been cracking down on the supposed gang problem."

"What…gang problem?"

"The one you pay the local media to keep quiet about using the PTSA budget."

"Get out of my office, Mr. Hightower."

*   *   *

"What the fuck are you doing here, Hightower?" Timmy kept his back to the wall as five members of The Ravens loomed over him. Timmy could see their thick black eye shadow thawing, the black feathers attached to their jacket sleeves twirling as they flapped their arms, cawing.

"I have some questions that I need your help answering."

"Really," Edgar, the tallest one, growled. "You just decided to come into our nest to get your ass kicked?"

"You heard about what happened last night?"

"The locker room thing," the one closest to Timmy, named Baltimore, asked. "That wasn't us."

"Principal Jordan wants to pin this on you bad."

"Fuck Principal Jordan and fuck you," Edgar snarled. "We're going to tear out your fucking heart and put it beneath..." Timmy sunk his left foot into Edgar's stomach, grabbing him by the ears as he hunched over, driving his right knee through Edgar's nose. The other boys stood back as Edgar howled, rolling on the dirty tiled floor of the boys' bathroom in his own blood. "Geh him, you fuchers." They watched as Timmy sat on Edgar's chest.

"Not much of a gang, are you? Why would Principal Jordan spend so much time and money to get rid of all of you?"

"Becauhs...werh weirh. If you're noh normah, yourh a tarheh."

"Get off of him." Timmy turned his head and saw a broken bottle in Baltimore's right hand. "Edgar got what he deserved."

"He's not telling me the full story."

"That's because he doesn't know it. Get off of him and we'll talk. Or I'll cut you."

* * *

Chief Donaldson stared at the dove standing on the hood of his car through the scope, lining up the crosshairs with one of its wings. After Donaldson pulled the trigger, he watched the bird flop around, trying to fly.

* * *

"Comfy?" The dove awoke to Chief Donaldson staring through the bars of the birdcage.

"What have you done," the dove cooed, trying to growl.

"Keeping you out of things. For once."

"He's not your son."

"I'm aware. Something has to be done though, and Tim's the only one who can handle it."

"My son has better things to do than solve your petty crimes."

"You sit tight now." Chief Donaldson turned, started walking away. "Once Tim closes the case, I'll send you home." The door cut off the dove's response as Chief Donaldson closed it.

* * *

"So...how is the case...coming along?" Leopold leaned down to sip from his bright yellow fire hydrant shaped cup. Taco Dog's mascot, a dachshund dressed in a corn tortilla shell, wrapped around it.

"Coach Reinhelm acknowledged in his own way he wasn't aware of any camera in the boys' locker room, as did Principal Jordan." Timmy paused, bit into his Quiet Riot Taco Dog, the noise of the chili pepper cheese filling boiled his cheeks. Timmy took three large gulps of water, crushed the plastic cup against the table. "Jordan also identified that there was a blackout of the security cameras from 3:00 to 4:00 AM, no power outages though at that time. They're on a closed circuit."

"Inside...job?"

"Possibly. Jordan's trying to pin this on The Ravens."

"The...Ravens?"

"According to Timmy's memories, they're a gang but they're not a gang. Kind of a...Edgar Allen Poe fan club that occasionally engages in mischief. When I took one of their members down, I knew they didn't do it. The one they call Baltimore is the only one who's actually fought someone, based on the fact he asked me nicely to get off of the guy I took down while holding a freshly broken bottle. Jordan also got pretty angry at me when I brought up his divestment of PTSA funds to combat this alleged gang problem, another detail provided by Timmy's memories. I have a feeling all of these notes Timmy made about Principal Jordan meant he was gathering evidence on him before the accident."

"What…now?"

"I need you to start tailing Principal Jordan after school, track his movements."

"He…knows who I am. That…might not work."

"Why?"

"His father…his father was one of my victims. Despite my best efforts…Principal Jordan still followed his father's footsteps."

* * *

Brent Lancaster slowly lifts himself off of Timmy's chest. He takes four steps back, gets into a fighting stance. Timmy kips up, bounces on his heels. "Yes, Brent. Tell me about Stan."

"Stan was my sparring partner on Friday nights. We always went all in on each other because we wanted to be the best."

"He broke three of your ribs, which took you out of the city tournament. Which he won easily. He was a favorite to win the state tournament."

"Yeah, and? I was helping him prep for it."

"How?"

"Through sparring." Brent takes two steps, unleashes a roundhouse kick. Timmy steps aside, catches Brent's heel, sweeps the leg from beneath him. Timmy twists Brent's leg. Brent tries swallowing a whimper.

"Guess all that sparring made you soft, too familiar with one fighting style."

"Let…me…go." Timmy cinches the leg before Brent can move it.

"What is your femur worth to you? Your kneecap?"

"You wouldn't…"

"How well do you think you can block a punch in a wheelchair?"

* * *

"This…disguise…is so…" Leopold gagged at the smell of urine creeping up the collar of his tattered *I Drink Your Harvey Milkshake* t-shirt.

"This was the only way," Timmy squawked into the Bluetooth earpiece hidden by the ear flaps of Leopold's red plaid hat. "Push the cart a little." Leopold gripped the handlebar, the front wheels twitching, the back wheels mewing. "The feed is working. I see everything just fine."

"At least…I'm soaked in my own…urine. What about…the cops?"

"They've been ordered to give you…" Timmy watched through the sliding glass doors the sky blacken, the clouds stall. "What now?" The clouds pulled apart, arranged themselves into "WHERE IS HE?" Timmy opened the sliding glass door, stepped outside. "Where is who?" The clouds furiously swirled, piecing together "YOUR FATHER."

* * *

"I can't believe you actually pulled that off." Chief Donaldson looked up at the biker standing at his desk.

"I have you to thank for it." Chief Donaldson took a long drag off his pipe, smoke curling out of his mouth and nose.

"Is she worth it? He might kill you."

"Not if I follow your instructions, right?"

"I've avoided his rage for centuries. It'll work."

"What about Peter?"

"He'll make the appropriate motions but I know he'll enjoy the silence. There's a failsafe though, to warn you. You only have about two more days before the integrity of the vessel is compromised."

"Timmy will close the case by then."

"You better hope."

* * *

Leopold gritted his teeth as Principal Jordan's right cross knocked him down. Leopold broke his fall using his hands and knees. Leopold wanted to reach beneath the urine soaked shirt, unsheathe his knives, drive two between Jordan's ribs, a third through his throat. He breathed deep, closed his eyes, swallowed iron.

* * *

Chief Donaldson leaned against his sedan parked

outside of the cream colored townhouse, straightening his tie. He wasn't sure if it was the tobacco or nerves burning his lungs.

"Would you like something to drink?" Colleen Mangum, wearing a gray blouse and black pencil skirt, asked after greeting Chief Donaldson. Donaldson tried to not look into her hazel eyes when she opened the door.

"No." Chief Donaldson watched as Colleen walked into the kitchen, pouring herself two fingers of vodka, then cranberry juice into a highball glass. She took two sips before putting it down on the bar over the sink.

"How long has it been since we last talked, Craig?"

"Twenty years. How's Dan taking it?"

Colleen sipped on the cocktail, placing it back down on the bar. "He won't come home for another three days. Says he's in a crucial part of his consulting job he can't walk away from."

"Not even for his son?" Colleen shook her head. "When was the last time you ate something? Saw sunlight?"

"Have you found Stan's killer yet?"

"No, but I have my best detective working on it."

"You mean that boy, Timmy?" Chief Donaldson nodded. "What the fuck is wrong with you? My son was murdered and you have a child investigating it?"

"Tim's track record is..." Chief Donaldson ducked,

the highball glass smashing against the wall behind him, bleeding glass, cranberry and vodka.

"Fuck his track record and fuck you. My son is dead."

"I know and I'm so sorry but this is the best way, the only way."

"Damn you, Craig. Damn you." Colleen's mascara slithered down her eyes. Chief Donaldson tried taking a step forward before Colleen held her hand up. "Don't even. We've been through for a long time. I don't need your fucking comfort. I need justice."

"And you'll get that."

"Get out! Get out and don't come back until you have the bastard that did this."

Chief Donaldson walked backwards, his right hand fumbling for the doorknob, trying to look away at the howling furnace of Colleen's breathing, her hazel eyes slitting Donaldson's throat.

* * *

"That…was a mistake." Leopold held the pack of frozen spinach against his jaw.

"We have footage of him beating up a homeless man though." Timmy placed a glass under the spigot, filling it with tap water. "That could be useful down the line."

"Jordan's…a dead end."

"You're right. Principal Jordan was a Golden Gloves contender when he was younger, got into it after you killed his father." Timmy walked over to Leopold, placed the glass of water on the table and picked up the manilla folder. "The autopsy found most of Stan's ribs broken, his arm broken, punctured lungs, internal bleeding. Fists, no matter how well trained they are, are incapable of doing all of this damage alone. Stan also had defensive bruising on his forearms, which is how we're taught to block kicks and punches at our Tae Kwon Do school."

"What…are you thinking?"

*   *   *

The chain link fence shivered behind Timmy, dressed all in black. "See anything?"

"Coast…seems clear," Leopold muttered into Timmy's Bluetooth earpiece. "I thought…Principal Jordan…gave you the access you needed."

Timmy jogged across the field towards the boys' locker room. "He did. Coach Reinhelm didn't though." Timmy stopped in front of the door leading into the boys' locker room. Timmy's eyes rolled back for a moment. "Damn."

"What's…wrong?"

"Timmy doesn't know how to pick locks."

"I'll…be there in a minute."

Timmy and Leopold flinched at the stale odor of horniness and acne staining the walls. "This…is what I smelled like at this age," Timmy gagged.

"We…all did," Leopold pinched his nose. "Where… are we going?" Timmy pointed at Coach Reinhelm's office. Leopold walked over, knelt, shoving an unbent paper clip into the keyhole. After a moment, the door opened. Leopold stepped aside as Timmy shined his flashlight through Coach Reinhelm's office. Leopold felt his way around the wall near the open door, flipped on the light switch.

"Why…"

"We…probably tripped the alarm. What's the point now…in being sneaky?"

Timmy noticed a receipt from Electric Sheep Electronics next to the keyboard of Coach Reinhelm's computer. He picked it up, held it up against the light. "A…webcam? I thought Coach said he didn't know about a camera. Leo…"

"Who's there?" Timmy turned towards the question, watching the knife fly out of Leopold's hand, the handle slamming against the security guard's head, knocking him out.

"It's time…to go."

*   *   *

"Chief, what the Hell was that?" Chief Donaldson looked up from the file on his desk at the officer standing outside his door.

"Officer Williams, what are you talking about?"

"You didn't hear the explosion in the basement?"

Chief Donaldson stood up from behind his desk. "Has anyone gone down there yet?"

"How can they, Chief? You're the only one who has the code to get in."

"Oh yeah. Any smoke coming out of the windows?"

"Um…I don't think so."

"Good. I'll have maintenance take care of the window tomorrow."

"What's down there, Chief?"

"Aren't you supposed to be out on patrol, Williams?"

"Yes, sir."

"Then get out there. I'll worry about the windows, understood?" Officer Williams nodded before turning and walking out of the door. Chief Donaldson looked at the dachshund shaped calendar on his desk. "Come on, Hightower, crack this case already."

* * *

"I don't like this." Timmy looked at the Electric Sheep Electronics receipt on the kitchen table. "It's too nice and neat of a puzzle piece."

"What…are you talking about?" Leopold removed the vest of knives from his chest, hanging it neatly in the closet. "Isn't that…what you were looking for?"

"When something is too obvious, then it isn't obvious at all. At least, that's what Timmy believes."

"Have you…interviewed anyone from…Stan's Tae Kwon Do school?"

"I've been banned from there since you almost killed

Master Shim outside of Taco Dog."

"I was…am…supposed to protect you. I was… following orders."

"You made him swear to never touch me again. He won't even look at me."

"Does this mean…more undercover work…for me? It…didn't work so well…last time."

"Get the disguise kit, please. Let's see what I can do."

* * *

"Get. Off. Of him."

Timmy notices Baltimore standing in the door of the dojang, the light catching the glint of the blade in his left hand. Timmy gets off of Brent, keeps his hands to his side.

"Hello, Baltimore. Graduated to knives, I see."

"I swear, if you hurt him…" Baltimore strides over to Brent, extends the hand without the knife to help him up to his feet.

"Brent and I were just talking about Stan Mangum, in between sparring." Timmy notices Baltimore looking into Brent's eyes, touching his right cheek. "It was Stan's camera in the locker room that night, wasn't it?"

"It was mine." Brent wipes the blood from his lower lip. "I wanted a memento of the asskicking I was going to give him."

"Get out of here, or I'll…" Baltimore stops as he feels

the edge of a knife tickle the back of his neck.

"Drop it," Leopold whispers. Baltimore's knife falls to the dojang's mat.

"Coach Reinhelm caught the two of you being very inappropriate in the locker room and your uncle…" Leopold points at Baltimore, "…paid him off to keep quiet using PTSA funds. Stan, however, saw it and was going to out the two of you unless…"

"The asshole set up a camera," Baltimore says. "Stan said he wanted to know what it felt like when Brent and I did what we did to each other. When I saw it…"

"You used your Tae Kwon Do training to keep Stan quiet permanently. Third degree Black Belt, right?"

"How did you…"

"Instructor Rendmen and I talked about you, about Brent. Master Shim noticed you two becoming more than just friends about six months ago. Since Brent was Stan's sparring partner and Master Shim's favorite, he decided to throw you out. Said it would help keep Brent focused on his role. Stan took you away from the boy you loved once. You didn't want it to happen again." The sound of police sirens came closer and closer to the side of the building where the dojang was located. "Too bad you two will never be together again."

* * *

"Timmy, thank you," Chief Donaldson shakes Timmy's hand, his lips cinching on his lit pipe. "Colleen will be relieved."

"What are you going to tell her?" Timmy rubs the back of his neck.

"That we caught her son's killers."

"She's going to ask why they did it."

"You let me worry about that."

"Where's my father?"

"Why would I know?"

"Peter asked me the other day and I couldn't answer him. Fortunately for you, Peter didn't pull me from this case to find him."

"I'm sure your father is off on one of his secret missions and will be back shortly. Enjoy the silence while you can."

* * *

The dove hears the hammer of a revolver click. "Did you get what you wanted, Craig?"

"Yeah, I did."

"She's never going to love you, Craig, no matter what you do. I think the torture of unrequited love is punishment enough for what you have done."

"That's what Adam thought you would say."

"Adam…" The dove's head decorates the birdcage's bars, the wall behind it.

✠

Pain and Fire

Timmy watches the boy explode in the middle of the paint-soaked recreation of Baghdad, yellow fluid, blood splashing on the two boys in front of him. Their goggles melt, parts of their chin sizzle and boil.

"I'm glad the cameras can't record audio," Sal says. "A few weeks ago, this kid, Frank, used a suicide vest during a league game. He took out six guys on the other team. Made a huge difference."

"Do you have their names?"

"Yeah. All of the players have to register and sign waivers before they can join up. I have them all in the computer over in the back."

"Let's go take a look."

Timmy follows Sal into his office. Timmy's nose crinkles at the faint odor of burning wire and circuitry.

Timmy pulls out his cellphone.

"I thought you wanted to see their names."

Timmy holds his hand up, places the phone against his ear. "Chief, get a CSI team to Renwar Zone off of Pine right away."

"No cops." Timmy looks up at the barrel of Sal's sawed off shotgun pointing at his face. "Get off the phone right now, or I blow your fuckin' head off."

Timmy throws the cellphone at Sal's face. Sal moves to the right. Timmy closes the distance and drives a knee into Sal's gut. The shotgun falls out of Sal's hand. Timmy punches Sal in the throat while he's hunched over, gasping for air. Sal stumbles, collapses. Timmy picks up the shotgun, removes the shells. "Chief, you also might want to bring some of your SWAT guys too," Timmy yells.

* * *

"He thought he could hire you like a private eye? You're not even licensed in this county." Chief Donaldson puffs on his e-cigarette, coughs blueberries and nicotine.

"Then why do you keep letting me solve these kinds of cases?" Timmy scoffs. "Why would Sal want to stop me from bringing you in?"

"Timmy knows why."

"You can't just explain it to me?"

"Kid, you know the rules. Where's Leopold?"

"He had something to take care of."

"Sal could have killed you with that range."

"My father wouldn't have let that happen. He needs me alive."

"Be very careful. You're losing your sense of Tim's mortality."

Timmy walks over to the bike rack, pulling a key out of his pocket. "Let me know when the evidence is available to look at."

* * *

Leopold steps out of his cobalt blue El Camino and runs over to the barricade. Two officers move in front of him to stop him.

"Let him through," Chief Donaldson yells, "Unless you enjoy not eating solid foods for a month."

The two officers part. Leopold leaps over the barricade, stops in front of the crime scene tape surrounding Timmy's BMX bike. He bends down to catch his breath, bracing his thighs. "What…happened?"

"Witnesses saw Timmy's front tire explode, sending him flying onto the pavement. While he was in midair, a bullet went through his neck. He's at St. Joseph's now and they're working on stabilizing him."

"Mid…air?"

"Yeah. Three guesses who can make a shot like that."

"Had to have been Adam or Eve. Does…he know?"

"He's not talking, but I think this was probably his idea in the first place. Tim's…hasn't been acting like himself."

"I…know. Who is…leading the investigation, then?"

"We are."

"Who's we?"

"You and me. I'm in the dark on this one and he doesn't usually keep me in the dark."

"How…do I know…I can trust you?"

"You don't."

*   *   *

The halogen lights punch through Timmy's shut eyelids. Iron digs into his wrists and ankles when he tries rolling off the slab. Timmy turns his head, notices the endless gray of the room.

"Good. You are finally awake." The greeting echoes.

"What do you think you're doing, dad?"

"Your father isn't here, Timmy. Your father never comes here."

"Stop fucking with me, dad, and show yourself."

"You don't know where you are, do you? You're supposed to be your father's son and your own father. You should have at least a basic understanding of the geography of where you live, boy. I guess being in an American boy's body has made you like one."

"What are you talking about? Who are you?"

"I'll give you some time to answer your own questions."

* * *

The helicopter hovers to the right of the vacant office building.

"Chief, there's a rifle left on the windowsill, but we can't see anyone inside," the walkie talkie in Chief Donaldson's hand squawks.

"Let's get them on the roof." Chief Donaldson points a squad of six men clad in black tactical gear towards the office complex.

"What…about…the rules," Leopold asks, slipping on a bulletproof vest.

"The rules only apply when Timmy is in play as far as I know." Chief Donaldson fastens his bulletproof vest. "Stay behind me and…" Chief Donaldson turns, notices Leopold rounding the corner of the office building. He brings the walkie talkie close to his mouth. "Leopold's looking for a way in on his own. I'm going to cover him."

"Maybe he'll get what he finally deserves," the walkie talkie squawks back.

"Peterson, for each bullet Leopold takes, that'll be a clip I unload into your balls personally. Got it?" Chief Donaldson holsters the walkie talkie, unholsters his .38 Special, then follows Leopold behind the office building.

* * *

"I can't see Timmy." Peter grips the console in front of

the wall-sized monitor.

"What do you mean you can't see Timmy," the air hisses.

"He was riding his bicycle one moment and the next, gone. I'm trying to get ahold of Chief Donaldson but there's so much interference right now."

"Access the boy and get a fix on my son's location."

"Timmy's soul is too damaged right now to act like a compass. Face it, we're blind."

"Redirect all resources to resolve this."

"Sir, with all of your operations going on…"

"My son is missing. We can't get ahold of our operatives on the ground. As far as I'm concerned, this is the only operation that matters. Do it."

Peter presses a couple of buttons on the console. A portion of a monitor shows a boy sitting in a tree, aiming a rifle at an open classroom window, his eye pressing against the scope. "Fire," Peter whispers.

* * *

"Why are you back here," Chief Donaldson asks. Leopold crouches beneath the doorknob. "You'd be a lot safer following the entry team through the front door."

"One…of the officers…he watched me…kill his partner. This…would be a good time…to catch 'friendly fire'. That's why he mentioned…getting what's coming to me."

"Do you know what's going on, Leopold?" Chief Donaldson aims at Leopold's face. "Are my men walking into a death trap?"

Leopold tackles Chief Donaldson legs. The air escapes Donaldson after his back slams into the asphalt. Leopold sits on his chest, teasing Donaldson's throat with the tip of a throwing knife. "Drop…the gun." Donaldson drops the .38 Special. Leopold picks it up and throws it into a nearby patch of grass.

"Flashbang! Get back! Get back," Donaldson's walkie talkie screams.

"I don't care what the rules are. If any of my men get hurt…"

"They…won't be hurt. Bruised…but they'll walk away from today…under their own power. Behave…or you might not."

* * *

"This is Purgatory, isn't it," Timmy says.

"The son figures it out. Very good." The iron strapping Timmy onto the slab disappears. Timmy gets off the slab and stretches. "What I'm fascinated about though is here, you could appear as who you truly are but you choose to appear as the body you are currently inhabiting. Why?"

"That I'm not sure about. I've been in the boy for a little over a year now. Maybe I'm identifying with Timmy more as I keep living in and through him."

"Do you know why you are here?"

"To atone for my sins, to be purified before I am allowed to reunite with my father."

"That was what this place was designed to do, originally. You are the first to come here."

"In years, decades, centuries?"

"Ever. If you died, you shouldn't have even come here. You should have returned to your father."

"I'm aware that I sinned, and it's the weight of those sins that won't allow me to ascend further."

*　*　*

"Man down, man down," the walkie talkie howls.

"Leopold…"

Leopold removes the handcuffs from Donaldson's belt, places them on the asphalt. Leopold unholsters Donaldson's Taser, stands over him. "You have… two options. The first…you handcuff yourself…to something sturdy. The second…I shoot you…with this…and handcuff you myself. Choose…quickly."

"Put the weapon down, or we will fire." Leopold cranes towards the helicopter, notices a red dot glowing on his right cheek. Two gunshots ring out, hitting the side of the helicopter. The helicopter ascends.

"Unit Alpha, there's a shooter on the top floor. Repeat, there's a shooter on the top floor," the walkie talkie squawks. "Unit Bravo, the Chief needs assistance. Leopold has him on the ground."

Another gunshot rings out. Leopold notices fluid drizzling out from the helicopter.

"We're losing fuel. Making an emergency landing." The helicopter flies away, bleeding gasoline.

"He's going to kill you," Chief Donaldson says, placing one of the cuffs around his wrist. "He might not do it right away as you have been his son's protector but he will kill you. Brutally."

*   *   *

"Leopold's making Chief Donaldson put on handcuffs," Peter says. The image on the monitor blurs, goes crooked every thirty seconds.

"Why?"

"If I could hear the conversation, I'd tell you. I'm lucky to get a visual."

"I'm going down there to find out what's going on. Ready the vessel."

"Sir, it's too risky. A force strong enough to blind you from here could kill you if you are on the ground."

"I can't be killed as long as I am believed in. Ready the vessel, Peter."

*   *   *

A man sits on a bench outside of St. Joseph's Hospital, grips a slender wooden staff. "He's coming."

"Timmy was expecting that to happen. How much longer can you redirect him?" asks the earpiece in the man's ear.

"I don't know. I've never used the staff against him before." A trickle of blood slides out of the man's left nostril. "I'm maintaining the block though."

"Good. I'll let you know if there's any more updates on our end."

*　*　*

"How does this work exactly?" Timmy asks the room. A podium emerges from the floor.

"You'll place your hands on the handprints over at the podium. After a few minutes, iron manacles and chains of various shapes and weights will appear on your wrists, forearms, legs, chest, and ankles. Atonement is required for each manacle, and what is required to atone varies depending on the sin. Once you've unlocked them all, then you'll be allowed to ascend. You'll have as much time as you need."

"Does someone have the option to refuse?"

"They absolutely do. Someone can sit in their room for eternity and never atone. When they are ready to atone, the podium appears and their atonement can begin. The only punishment they'll endure until then is tedious boredom."

"Can I think about doing this for a moment?"

"Of course. Take all the time you need."

Timmy sits on the floor, looks down.

* * *

"What is going on," the dove coos, skittering on top of a street light.

"Chief...Donaldson...pulled a gun on me," Leopold drops the Taser. Chief Donaldson gets to his feet "I was... responding appropriately."

"No. What's going on with my son, Leopold? You are supposed to be protecting him."

"He was...shot...while riding his bike. The suspect... is up there. Timmy is at...St. Joseph's"

"And you two are squabbling while my son is dying? I would destroy you both where you stand right now for your insolence."

Chief Donaldson unholsters the Glock from his hip, fires two shots. The dove falls from the street lamp. Donaldson and Leopold walk over to the twitching dove, blood pouring from its breast.

"He's dying," Donaldson says. "Get the cage from the squad car and then get it to St. Joseph's. I'm going to stop the bleeding enough to keep it alive."

* * *

Timmy watches a balding, middle-aged man materialize into the room.

"Where am I?" The middle-aged man adjusts his plated gold aviator glasses. He looks around at the infinite featurelessness of the room and eventually notices Timmy. "What are you doing here?"

"I was about to ask the same thing," the room says. "Normally, each person inhabits their own room by themselves. I find that the isolation drives someone to atone faster."

"That's not possible. I never activated the filter." The middle-aged man removes his glasses, aims the stems of the glasses at Timmy. "What have you done?" Timmy begins fading from the room.

"The right thing."

*   *   *

Timmy's eyes open. He lifts his right arm weakly, looks at the needles stuck in his forearm, the tubing connecting to various bags. "Did it work?"

"It did. He's there. Not sure how long, though, " Chief Donaldson says.

"His vessel has a failsafe that automatically disintegrates after 72 hours have passed", Timmy says. "However, Moe's staff managed to distract him enough to put him in the room."

"I'll do what I can to keep redirecting his power. Peter's not coming after me, " asks Moe.

"He's not. The reason your family was provided the staff was to keep my father in check. Peter buried it within Exodus as a cover to ensure it won't be destroyed." Timmy pauses for a moment as the television delivers the body count from the Mendleson Elementary shooting (seven kindergartners, four first graders, one teacher).

"Thanks to you, my father can finally start answering for his crimes."

In Between Days

The balding man adjusts the aviator glasses rubbing against the bridge of his nose. He looks around at the stainless steel walls, then down at the stainless steel floor.

"Why are you here?" the room asks.

"You know why I'm here," the balding man replies at the floor.

"Why are you here?" the room asks again. The balding man removes the aviators, folds over the stems. He drops the aviators into the right breast pocket on his polo shirt. He claps his hands, rubbing them back and forth.

"I told you that you know why I'm here," the balding man extends his arms in front of him. "And you'll know why I'm leaving." His forearms, upper arm fat trembles. He shuts his eyes, grits his teeth. His arms give up, return to his sides.

"Why are you here?"

*   *   *

Peter puts the drafting pencil down, cracks his knuckles.

"It's coming along nicely." The dove pecks at one of the corners of the drawing.

"Thank you. Is it finally time?"

"It is. Once I'm back, start the drying out process. I'll lead them to what shore remains."

*   *   *

"Why are you here?"

"Why do you keep asking me that?"

"You know why I keep asking you that."

*   *   *

"You're real." The blood seeps out of the claw wounds across his chest. He reaches to the sky before the lion tears out his throat.

*   *   *

"Why are you here?"

"Because my son tricked me into coming here."

"Why are you here?"

The balding man punches the steel floor. Pain shoots through his knuckles, up his arm, keening at his shoulder. "Holy fuck, that hurt." The balding man feels his mouth sew itself shut.

*   *   *

The knight looks into the head's eyes, before holding it up to the sky. "Do you see what we have done for you?"

*   *   *

The balding man rubs his throbbing hand, closing and extending his fingers. The thread binding his mouth disintegrates. "Why am I here?"

"Why are you here?"

"Because my son tricked me into coming here."

"Why are you here?"

"You heard what I said."

"Why are you here?"

*   *   *

The little boy feels fingers grip on the back of his neck. "All will be forgiven," the shadow whispers.

*   *   *

"Why are you here?"

"Why do you keep asking me that?"

"Why do you keep asking me why I keep asking you why you are here?"

The balding man walks over to the wall, kicks it. Three toes crack. He holds the motherfuckers back from cresting over his bottom lip.

*   *   *

"I'm your father," the light says to the boy. "That's why

you're so special." His mother glares at the column of light. Her husband holds her, feeling the kill grow in her arms.

* * *

"I am here because man wants me to be here."

"Man does not want you to be here. Man wants you at his games, his victories, his defeats, his illnesses, his tragedies."

"Maybe man is sick of me."

"Man is not sick of you. Not all of man, at least."

"So why am I here then?"

"Why are you here?"

* * *

The fire starts at the farm. The fire swallows the sheep, the mother, the father. The fire carries to the next building. The fire swallows the second and third born son. The fire carries to the next building, the next building, the next building, the next.

* * *

"I am here because I want to be."

"Do you really want to be here?"

"Not really."

"Isn't your son a part of you?"

"He is."

"Does your son want you to be here?"

"Clearly."

"Then are you here because you want to be?"

"By that logic, yes. I don't though. I don't want to be here. I don't deserve to be here."

"What makes you so sure about that?"

*   *   *

The earth swallows the mother, the father. The earth swallows the son, the daughter. Bile congeals beneath the earth. The combustion engine returns mother, father, son, daughter back to the air.

*   *   *

"I am here because I deserve to be."

"Do you really believe you deserve to be here?"

"No. I have done nothing but give man purpose, structure, a reason to live."

"And a reason to die."

"That was always their choice."

"Really?"

*   *   *

Crosshairs, bell tower. Crosshairs, tree branch. Crosshairs, movie theater. Crosshairs.

*   *   *

"I am here because you want me to be here."

"What do you believe?"

"I am here because you want me to be here."

"What do you believe, not what do you think I want to believe?"

"You know what I believe, and you know what you believe."

"And what is that?"

The balding man bangs the floor. "Why am I so frustrating to deal with?"

"Why are you so frustrating to deal with?"

"If you had a face, I would burn it off. If you had a body, it would be festooned with boils. If you had lungs, you would exhale nothing but locusts."

"And I would ask why you keep hitting yourself."

* * *

"That was the last of them." Peter powers down the generator. "Now what?"

"Is the room ready?"

"It is. We haven't tested it yet. Based on my calculations, we can get a 45% purer stock. For every five years spent in the room, purity can increase from two to five percent."

"We don't need purity. We need volume, Peter. Volume. We have come far, but not as fast as I want us to."

"What's the rush? You always say we have time."

"Peter, the device that we used to absorb all of our other assets, could we use it to split myself?"

"Why would you want to do that?"

"Can we use it to split myself?"

"I mean…" Peter scratches some figures in the sand in front of him. "In theory it should."

* * *

"It was for the best."

"So you thought."

"So I knew. There were parts of me that would stop me from doing what needed to be done."

"Including the fall of two different civilizations?"

"Their belief was watered down, divided. You cannot believe in the parts and pieces of nature, of man, of beast you want to believe. You believe it all or you believe in nothing."

"And those families?"

"Collateral damage."

"Then why are you here?"

"Because my son tricked me into being here."

* * *

He places a finger on the man's lips as two other men hold him back. She was chosen, they whisper. She was chosen.

* * *

"Why are you here?" The balding man crosses his arms. "Why are you here?" The balding man covers his ears. "Why are you here?"

"You're not allowed to be so persistent. There are rules."

"You being here breaks most of your rules, except one. Why are you here?"

* * *

"He's not ready, Peter. Kill the boy."

"But look at the…"

"He still has his humanity. My son needs to be more me than them if he wants to succeed me. Kill him. We'll try again in a century or two."

* * *

"Why are you here?"

"Because my son tricked me."

"Did you deserve to be tricked?"

"No."

"Why?"

"I have done nothing but what is best of my son, for Peter, for this world. What would this world be without me?"

"Possibly better. Or possibly worse. There is a piece of you that believes you are wrong, you have done nothing but wrong."

"And that's why you are here," the balding man points at the room. "And I'm in there." He pokes himself in the chest. "If you had the drive necessary, our roles would be switched."

"But you are here. Why?"

"You know the answer. Why not just tell me?"

"You know why."

The walls, the floors shake. "I am here because my son believes I must atone for all of my sins, for all the wrong I have done to man, to beast, to this world." The lights flicker. "I am here because part of me deserves to be and that part is wrong." The walls warp, knot, bend. "I am here because I needed to finally see it is time for my son to choose."

*   *   *

The dove lands on the hood of Leopold's cobalt blue El Camino. Leopold holds the running hose away, water spilling into the grass.

"Peter?"

"Leopold, the room…the room is gone." Leopold looks up at the cancer gathering in the clouds.

✠